BEING YOUNG CAN BE DANGEROUS

COUGER

When Your Being Haunted

III

A Novel

Billie Dureya Shell

COUGER III

Front Cover Image By graphic designer
Billie Dureyea Shell & Kenny Writes

First Printing Edition 2021

ISBN 978-1-7373922-3-1

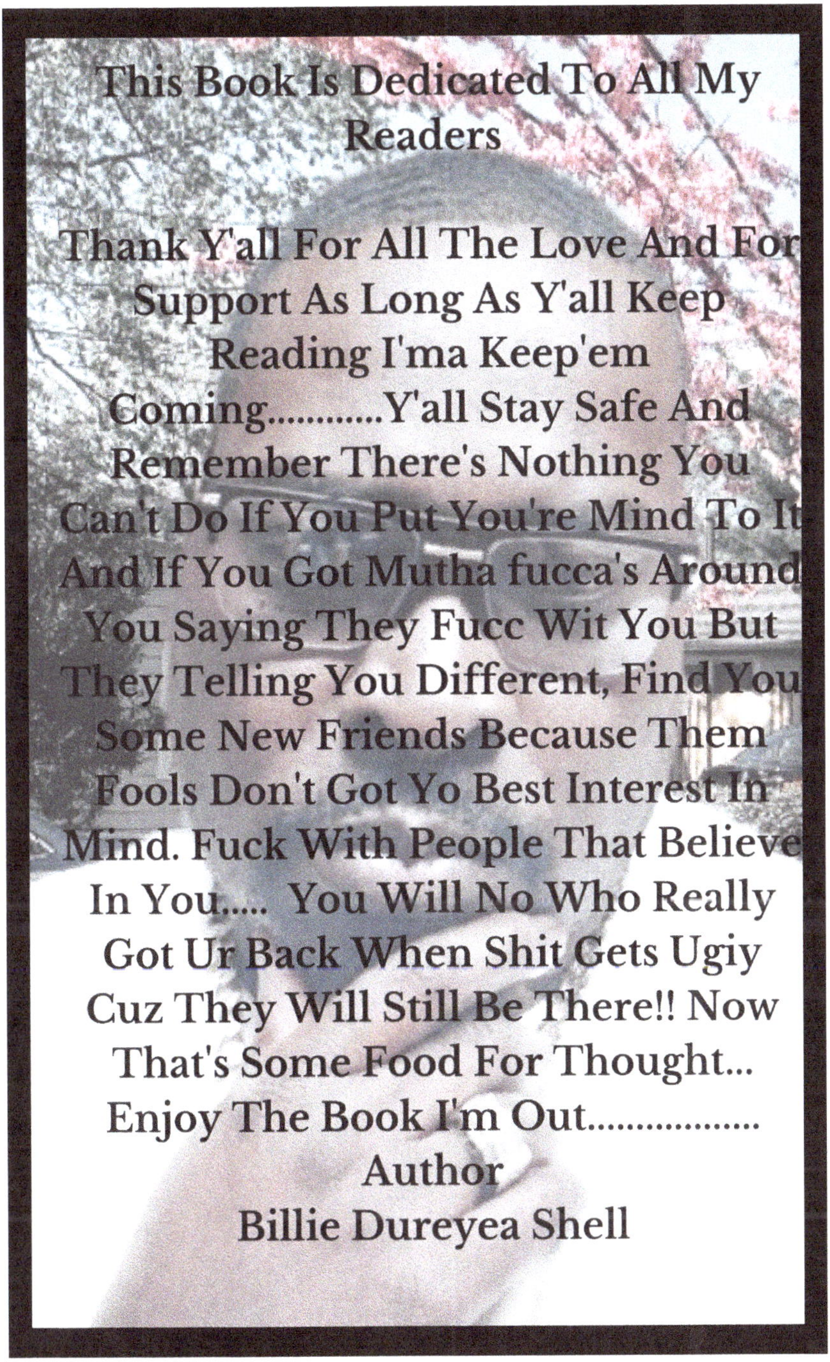

This Book Is Dedicated To All My
Readers

Thank Y'all For All The Love And For
Support As Long As Y'all Keep
Reading I'ma Keep'em
Coming.............Y'all Stay Safe And
Remember There's Nothing You
Can't Do If You Put You're Mind To It
And If You Got Mutha fucca's Around
You Saying They Fucc Wit You But
They Telling You Different, Find You
Some New Friends Because Them
Fools Don't Got Yo Best Interest In
Mind. Fuck With People That Believe
In You..... You Will No Who Really
Got Ur Back When Shit Gets Ugiy
Cuz They Will Still Be There!! Now
That's Some Food For Thought...
Enjoy The Book I'm Out.................
Author
Billie Dureyea Shell

ACKNOWLEDGEMENT

First and foremost I have to give honor to My Lord And Saviour Jesus Christ without him now of this would be possible. 2020 was a MUTHA FUCCA Corona Virus made shit hard 4 niggas but we made it threw y'all keep your head up and know that God got us, no matter they throw in our way no one can stop what God has plan for you…
Its 2021 now FUCC 2020 and Covid 19…. Now to my family momma I love you and you no I got you no matter what. You mean the world 2 me oh and NO MORE PINCHING LOL. To my little sister Glenda I love you blackie, you No I Got You always

To my Wife Shatoya Shell you get on my damn nerves ⬢ but I wouldnt trade you 4 anything In the world I love ♥ you more then words can ever express. To all my children I love y'all Jazmine, Ant'Tuan, Davon, Anthony, David, Lil Dureyea, Alura, Queen Diavion, Cameron, Preniece, Shaniece and Tajh I love u all and I'll 4ever have ur back you all give me a reason 2 smile… to my cousin Zane RIP nigga I miss u more then anyone will ever no, your always remembered love you bro. to my cousin Ty I miss you thank 4 looking out 4 me and Zane you played a big part in my life and I always looked up to you I love you… Uncle Woody I miss you and love you, you no your my favorite uncle… To my nigga Jamal love you, my brothers Lawrence and fred thank 4 showing me the game I love yall 4 that. To my oldest sister Nedra love you thank you 4 always having my back. to my family uncles anties cousins etc.. I love y'all even those of you that act funny as fuck

To my dark side niggas y'all no what it is YAAH GANG....
Now to all my readers and fans I love you thanks for reading I
hope u enjoy this book as much as I enjoy writing
them with this Corona Virus 19 shit there ain't shit to do but
write so I'm on my shit with that being said y'all be safe cover
your face and love each other life is short so love the ones that
really love I'm gone no. enjoy the book

STAY SAFE

Author Billie Dureyea Shell

THERE'S NOTHING U CANNOT DO

IF U PUT UR MIND 2 IT.

All you nigga's got EDD money so aint no excuse

why you can't get a book LOL

CHAPTER ONE

Damn, my head hurts. Groggy as hell, I slowly peeled my eyes open and watched the ceilin' spin. No, it's a ceilin' fan slowly rotating. Confused, I stared at it a moment, tryin' to remember what happened. Nothin' but poundin' temples. Slowly sittin' up, I looked dazedly around; plain white walls in a windowless room, that kinda looked like it used to be a storage closet. My foot kicked somethin' and my mouth dropped as a roll of tissue fell over and rolled towards a mop bucket. Tha fuck?! "Where tha hell am I?" Came out soundin' dry and raspy. Pullin' up to my feet, I walked over to a door, gripped knob and gave a twist, then again. Locked. Tha shit was locked! "Think Taylor, what's the last thing you remember?" I asked myself while leanin' against tha door. Bits and pieces ran through my mind like a freshly opened 500 piece puzzle poured on the table. I remembered Glenda comin' over 'cause she hadn't heard from Dove and was worried. I stiffened. Glenda! I was wit' Glenda, was she here too? Another thought popped in, we'd gone over to Dove's; whom I thought was probably gettin' banged by as many dicks as possible. Only, when we got there, Dove's place was trashed. And then what? Slammin' my eyes shut, I concentrated so hard I didn't even realize I'd moved until I ran into tha damn wall. "Ouch, fuck!" I would've kicked it but I didn't have on any shoes. My shoes! Them mafuckas cost me three hundred and fifty bucks on sale. Somebody was askin' for it! Okay, okay, focus Tay'; fuckin' focus. Throbbin' temples be damned, I needed to know where tha fuck I was and how I got here. Oh yeah, and where was Glenda and Dove. * I don't know how many hours I sat in that room/closet 'til I caved and used tha bucket to pee. Talk about humiliated, all I needed was a camera in my face recordin' my squat. Ooo, it's on when I find tha culprit; ain't gone be no fuckin' talkin'! Hungry and thirsty, I hope whoever did this hurries up and shows wit' some fuckin' nourishment before I waste away; losin' my shape in tha process. I wonder if anyone's lookin' for me, probably not. Which meant I'd have to help me myself. * Stomach growlin', throat dry, hands sore from poundin' against tha door; I lay curled in a ball fantasizin' 'bout layin' on a tropical island bein' catered to by a bunch of oiled up, buff, loin cloth wearin' gawds caterin' to my every whim. Tha shit was so real I swear I smelled chicken soup. My eyes snapped open in time to see a steamin' bowl bein' slid into the closet/room before tha door slammed closed. A lock clicked loudly in tha silence. Too weak to stand, I crawled over to said bowl, tossed tha spoon, picked up tha bowl and drank it down; chokin' on bits of chicken and noodles in my haste to put nourishment in my stomach. After awhile, I started namin' and singin' TV show theme songs to keep my sanity; like from Sanford & Son. Redd Foxx as Fred Sanford was hilarious and Kung Fu. Then I hummed tha Jefferson's which was another favorite, that Sherman Hemsley was pretty funny. Finally, tha door opened and in walked a behemoth of a man wearin' jeans, steel toed construction boots and tee shirt; his peanut shaped head void of hair. "Who are you? Where am I?" "Get up and put this on." he ordered, ignorin' my questions. Glancin' down, I saw he'd tossed me one a them eye masks people use to block out light when tryin' a sleep. "How 'bout no." Dude just stood there, like he's stuck on stupid waitin' on me. So I played tha waitin' game too. Fuck dat, I need to see where tha fuck I am. Dude sighed and said, "We can do this easy, where you walk on your own or I can knock yo ass out and carry you. Yo choice." Frownin', I sized his ass up right quick. At least six three, and bigger than Dwayne 'the Rock' Johnson and Ving Rhames put together; just too damn big for no reason. Damn dick probably shriveled to raisin status. I'm just sayin'. Crackin' ashy knuckles on hooves sized hands, dude snatched my collar, yanked me up and shook me so hard my brain rattled. Slappin' the eye mask on, I felt pain explode in my jaw before darkness claimed me. "Good, you're awake." said a voice I immediately recognized. Larry Love. I laughed. "Fucks so funny?" "You nigga. You that desperate where you had to snatch me up?" I snorted. "Fuckin' pitiful." I knew I sat tied to a chair, 'cause I could feel ropes bindin' my ankles and wrists. Suddenly tha mask was yanked off, followed by a hard slap. Blood tinged my lip so I licked it off. "Yum, what else you got?" Larry frowned. "That cocky game you playin' won't last long once you start yo new job." Smirked Larry, wishin' he had a camera to snap her face once he delivered the coup de gras. "If yo stupid ass don't untie me, tha first chance I get I'll slit yo fuckin' throat." I coolly told him, meanin' every word. Another slap. "Yeah, yeah. That won't be happening no time soon." Larry lit a Black & Mild, inhaled then blew smoke right in my face, the switch jiggled. "Ooh I'm so scared Taylor." Larry fake shivered. "Please don't kill me. I think you got it backwards, you'll be the one wishin' for death after a thousand or more niggas run all up in yo ass, bitch." A bad feelin' swept over me. "That's right bitch, welcome home. Welcome to The Dark Cavern hoe house."

CHAPTER TWO

I gave up on tryin' to figure out how long I'd been here and was now focused on findin' a way out. From closet/room to tied up in a chair, I still talked hella shit to Larry Love every time I saw his face. In his anger, he let it slip that I wasn't tha only one here; and that soon we'd all be sellin' our bodies for cash. I also found out I'd been there three weeks when I told Larry that someone would come lookin' for me. That bastard laughed so hard, tears ran down his face. It's all good, cause Taylor knows how to play too. I started yellin' and screamin'. My ass is sick of this fuckin' chair, I'm hungry and though I hate to admit it, I stink to high heaven since I haven't touched water since snatched. I thought I heard someone else yellin' too, but I wasn't sure. Tha lock clicked and the door swung open, smackin' tha wall. I knew someone was there though no one said anythin'. Tuggin' at the rope around my ankles alerted me whoever it was had crossed tha floor. Then my hands were freed, so I automatically reached up to remove face mask; only to cry out in pain when two of my fingers were squeezed and bent back, damn near touchin' finger to knuckles I'm sure. "Ow! Okay, okay!" Hand throbbin' I awaited orders on what he or she wanted. A hand gripped my arm and tugged, so I stood up and was led from tha room. Minutes later, even though I struggled, four hands divested me of all clothin' and doused my ass wit' freezin' shower water. A bar of soap was slapped in one hand, a thin ass rag in another. I felt like dis chick name Courtney who used to live in Dove's building last summer, 'cause I couldn't see shit and had to rely on other senses. So far I learned besides Larry's ass, there was another man who always smelled of peppermint candy and two chicks. I knew this cause both them dyke bitches always copped feels, their hands were too soft to be a man's. Fuckin' hoes on my list too. "Time," a voice grunted, scarin' me from my thoughts. A rough ass towel was tossed in my face, shit felt like it was peelin' skin as I dried off. Bein' sneaky, I dried my face, liftin' tha mask slightly so I could get a glimpse of one of these hoes. Reba! Clenchin' teeth, I quickly stuck my arm out, towel in hand to let 'em know I'm done; while debatin' on whether I make a move now, or wait. Towel yanked from my grip, both captors took an arm and walked me naked a few paces before shovin' me in a room, then lockin' me inside. Snatchin' off mask, I took in eight twin beds, all empty; while one held bedding, a pair of shorts and a faded white tee shirt. Givin' a sniff, I slowly slid on tha shorts since no panties or bra were in sight, then pulled on tha shirt which was snug as hell. There were two windows; the inside covered by wire used in chicken coops, the outside by bars; that eliminated exit by window. Fuck! Nothin' on tha walls to use as a weapon, no lamp or table. The door unlocked; I jumped to my feet heart racin'. A young white girl, around maybe eighteen or nineteen wit' fiery red hair on head and snatch was shoved inside; followed by a rolled mattress, which unfurled as tha door closed, revealin' pillow, blanket and tha same outfit I wore. Wet hair dripped trails of water down her back where they raced each other towards an ass so flat I told myself once we made it out, I'd hook her up wit' Dr. Crawford's number. "Hey." she greeted; finally coverin' her 40C's and hairy cat. "Sup." I returned dryly, idly wonderin' what's her story. "I'm Hannah, what's your name?" "Tay'." Short and sweet boo, cause I ain't here to make friends. "Any idea where we are, or how we got here?" Damn, chatty Hannah! Don't chu see my ass on lock just like you? Fuck outta here. I thought. "Sorry, that was a stupid question." she said. Amen sista'. "I still don't know how I ended up here. One minute I'm at the bus station asking for change," Uh no boo, get it right, it's called beggin' okay. "And the next, I woke up locked in a storage closet." My ears perked up. "Do you remember who you spoke to before wakin' up here?" Hannah frowned a minute, then gave a wide smile like her answer would win her money on Jeopardy. "Yeah, yeah, I do. It was some black lady. She asked me was I a runaway, and if I was hungry. I told her yes, I'm from Wyoming. I'd run away from my abusive, rapist step father and sure, I could eat. She flashed a bunch of cash and offered to take me to...shit, I can't remember. Anyway, I got in the front seat, we pull off and someone pops up from the backseat; slapped a rag over my face and voila, here I am." Hannah scooped up mattress, pillow and blanket then chose the empty bed closest to mines. I hope dis air head don't think we 'bout to be tha best of fuckin' friends, just cause I asked her ass a question. 'Cause it ain't happenin' okay. Layin' down I stared at water stained ceilin' wonderin' if Glenda and Dove would be next to be shoved into tha room. "Psst, psst." My eyes shot open. Damn, I don't even remember fallin' asleep, but darkness had fallen. "What." I snapped, ready to flip tha script if her ass woke me for somethin' stupid. "Listen." A scream rang out. "Omg, you hear that?" Duh, hell yeah I hear that! Again a scream rang out. Since we had no lights, I didn't know Hannah was cryin' til I heard snifflin'. "Tha fuck is you cryin' fo'?!" I yelled. "Shut tha hell up befo' they hear yo crybaby ass and they come in here!"

"Sorry....I'm sorry, I'm just so scared. Can I....can I get in bed wit' you....please?" Hannah loudly whispered. Rollin' eyes, I retorted wit' a, "Hell naw, fuck I look like. Now pull it togetha' fo' I smack the fuck out chu." The door swung open, hallway light spilled in tha room. Every time tha door opened my eyes would spring to our captor who always wore a ski mask, completely obliteratin' any chance of knowin' who they were. A muffled 'oompf' sounded when she was shoved in tha room so hard she crashed to tha floor; wackin' knees and elbows on tha hard linoleum. Hannah stumbled from bed, I guess to offer assistance to tha girl still lyin' on tha floor cryin'. My teeth ground togetha', cause I'm in a room wit' a buncha fuckin' crybabies I swear. Two shadows rose from tha floor just as the door opened and a rolled up mattress flew in, conkin' ole gurl in tha back. She in turn fell against Hannah and both went down. Fuckin' Three Stooges minus one, da fuck! Just before tha door closed I quickly asked, "Please, I beg you. May I have somethin' to drink?" Almost chokin' on my damn tongue to force it out soundin' all sugar and nice. Tha door slammed wit' no reply. Suckin' teeth, I flopped back in bed glad Hannah and whoever were quiet. Tha door opened and a small Styrofoam cup appeared. Shootin' from bed I almost bussed my ass on what felt like a piece of clothin'. "Thank you so much, bless you."

Jeezus if I keep it up I'ma hurl big chunks. Takin' cup, the door closed, then locked. Since I couldn't see, I sniffed the cup, then took a cautious sip; memories of Dove spikin' my drink dancin' in my head. Orange juice, and it was nice and cold. Even so, I only took anotha' sip, then sat on my bed and waited to see what reaction I'd have before drinkin' anymore. "Tay' this is Sophie, she's eighteen and from Hartford as well." So. Fuck I look like, tha city takin' a census!? These bitches gone make tha switch flip and it ain't gone be pretty okay. 'Cause I gotta lotta tension I'm dealin' wit' and I don't have tha patience fo' tha bull. I'm just sayin'. Mornin' came grey and listless. I had to twist my frame all crazy just to see the sky through all tha crap blockin' tha window. The view was nothin' but grass and trees as far as tha eye could see. I couldn't even tell if this was tha front of the building or not. Hannah yawned, then stretched wit' a bunch of bones crackin'. "Mornin' Tay', Sophie." she greeted. "Sup," Hannah snorted. "You don't say much hunh?" Sophie rolled over, farted, then sat up, big owl like eyes focused on me. "I talk when I've got shit to say." Leavin' tha window I walked back over to my bed, bent and scooped up my orange juice. I'd left a drop in it last night, but this mornin' tha fuckin' cups bone dry. "A'ight let's get shit straight right damn now, if I have somethin' and don't offer to share, don't wait til I'm sleep to get sticky fingers, 'cause you'll get beat da fuck down!" I snapped, switch jigglin'. "Sorry, thought it was for all of us." said Sophie. I glared at this dumb bunny and flipped. "Listen here Sophie, did yo wailin' ass ask for a drink last night? No, 'cause you was too damn busy cryin'. Did Hannah ask? No. So how tha fuck you got share outta me bein' tha only one to speak up? I don't know nor care, all I know is you touch my shit again and it's yo ass, understand!?" I loudly exclaimed. Sophie stood, blinked and gone say, "Omg, it was barely a sip. Must you people always blow things way outta proportion." Ooo, no she didn't throw out tha 'you people' card. Droppin' cup, I marched right up in her space, hummin' breath and all. "Listen you redneck, backwoods, country, road kill eatin' bitch. You don't know me boo, you comin' at me like you want me to snatch yo ass one good time." I chest bumped her. "I dare yo ass to say anotha' word, racist or nah!" Sophie quickly glanced at Hannah so my head followed; 'cause we all know 'them people' stick togetha', but Hannah was still beside her bed. Before my head finished turnin', Sophie reached out and slapped me. Ballin' a fist, I returned her serve wit' a punch to them racist ass, juice drinkin' lips followed by anotha to an eye, then I shoved her ass. Tha back of her legs hit tha bed followed by Sophie fallin' on and off on the opposite side. Breathin' hard cause adrenaline's flowin' and I thought wit' all that mouth she'd give me some exercise. I glared at Sophie, picked up my cup and tossed it at her. Sophie lay on tha floor, cryin' like I'd attempted murder and she'd barely escaped. Hoe please. Dustin' my hands on lightweight, I strode back to my bed, peepin' how Hannah stared at me in awe. That's right boo, now you know Taylor ain't nothin' to fuck wit', no matter if it's orange juice or a fuckin' corner slice of bread.

CHAPTER THREE

This time after showers, we were givin' toothbrushes. Brushin' neva felt so good! One of tha guards asked Sophie what happened to her lip. I hadn't hit her hard enough to cause a black eye, but her lips were puffy like she'd just left from havin' collagen injections. I silently dared her ass to look my way or mutter my name. She's smarter than I thought cause she lied and said that it happened when tha guard pushed her in tha room last night. Then it was back to our room where breakfast waited on our beds, which consisted of two eggs, waffles, a boiled egg, two slices of bacon and a small pint of milk like they served at school lunch. Just to be funny, I demanded Sophie give up her milk, which she did without a protest. Everything we ate wit' was plastic; they gave us a plastic spork, tha bowl holdin' eggs was Styrofoam along wit' paper plate. Once done and they came to collect our trash a spork was missin'. It was obvious it was Sophie, who they dragged out kickin' and screamin'. Hannah sat tremblin' while I had to give ole gurl props for havin' tha courage to try. Hours later tha door opened and in strut this tall ass chick wit' a Mohawk. Hannah, always tha host, quickly introduced herself. "The names Sharon." she said wit' a thick ass accent. "Oh." gushed Hannah. "I love your accent, where are you from?" "The Bahamas, but I haven't been home in ages." said Sharon. Sharon was a'ight if you like 'em tall. She was definitely curvy and had sultry grey eyes. "And what's your name?" Before I could answer, Hannah replied, "That's Tay'. She was here before any of us." "For the record sweetie, I asked Tay'. She can talk right?" I smiled. Ooo, I like dis tall bitch. "Sorry." Of course you are boo; and if yo ass don't toughen us, yo ass ain't gonna surive. Sophie returned some time durin' tha night, wakin' everybody wit' her damn cryin'. "Oh my gosh!" I yelled. "Enough of tha cryin', did they break yo arm? Shove a broom up yo ass and you carryin' 'round a bunch of damn splinters? No, so shut tha hell up before I give you a reason!" "Thank you!" said Sharon. "Finally someone who sees shit my way." "They..they beat me." Sniff, sniff. "Then raped me." Sharon burst out laughin'. "Is that all? Girl shut up and grow a backbone." Now I laughed. "Ump I was thinkin' tha exact same thing." "Shut up!" Sophie screamed. "I was a virgin and they raped me! How can you p..women laugh at that?!" Ole

Sophie sounds like she's on goin' Crazy Lane headed for Nervous Break Down Avenue. Smirk. Sharon snorted. "All I know is I'm tryin to sleep. So suck that shit up, dry yo snotty face and go to damn sleep. Last warning chica." Growled Sharon. Sophie did as ordered; but not before crossin' tha room and climbin' in bed wit' Hannah. Hygiene taken care of, we trudged back to our room to find two more chicks sittin' atop beds; one white, one black and both looked like they'd been on the loosin' end of a brawl. I sniffed. Sharon frowned and snarled, "Who smells like Chicken of the Sea on wheat toast?" Neither girl said a word. "I know you ugly hoes heard me." The black girl who was well beyond black spat a "Fuck you." while the white girl kept her eyes low. Sharon smiled. "Maybe later once you scrub yo snatch homie, cause you foul." Yess! Serve her fishy ass a side of tartar sauce and fries boo! "So what are your names?" Asked Hannah tryin' a break the tension. "I'm Rochelle." said dark meat. "And that's Linda." "I heard more girls across the hall. I tripped on purpose and got a quick look inside before they dragged us in here." mumbled Linda. All eyes turned on her. "And?" I said promptin' dis chick to open her trap and spill it. "Well there were at least six beds and all of 'em looked full. A short black guy was givin' 'em the house rules, something about opening day and what's expected." "And?" Said Sharon. Linda shrugged. "That's it, that's all I heard." We all eyed each other. "Do you think we'll get the same speech?" questioned a wide eyed Hannah. "Does yo face turn red when upset?" I snapped. "Hell yeah we're gonna hear tha speech. We'll be expected to fuck n suck fo' a buck. This is a hoe house and we are tha hoes. Damn, whatchu need, a house to fall on yo ass? This ain't Kansas boo and it ain't Oz either." Damn it felt good to let that shit out. The door swung open and in walked Larry Love who looked a lil taller. My eyes dropped, he had on black construction boots. Ump, don't catch a nosebleed boo. I'm just sayin'. Starin' right at me he gave a sickly grin. Nucca please. Yo short, stalkin' ass ain't doin' nothin' over here boo. Hell, you doin' me a favor okay; cause a bitch needed a break from Brandon and Joshua's mental asses, so try again. Shit didn't you know, Taylor loves tha dick boo. I need all the essential minerals and vitamins, I'm just sayin'. I blew Larry a kiss, his eyes widened. Ha! Sucka for tha nookie ass nigga! "A'ight listen up! Our employer has graciously deemed you lucky ladies the chance to turn yo lives around. You've been selected to work here to pleasure men and women if they so desire. You'll have more freedom once we see we can trust you." Larry stopped, then glanced at each girl before again starin' at me. What nucca, you want me to flash you a boob? Damn talk already, 'cause you gone make tha switch flip, okay. "Uh..yeah. So the more money you pull in, the more your stock rises, which in turn earns you certain perks. There's no way to escape. All doors and windows are secured and there'll always be security around. No ones lookin' for you, so get that thought outta yo heads. Any questions?" All hands went up. "Yeah the red head, sup?" Hannah nervously smiled. "Do we get to go outside once we earn perks?" "Fuck all that." cut in Sharon. "Do we get a cut for layin' on our backs and havin' sore jaws?" "Are we expected to fuck clients in this room?" Linda threw in. The questions kept comin' until exasperated, Larry yelled out, "shut up! Damn, do any of ya'll bitches have common sense?" He spat, muscle twitching in his jaw. "No you won't be allowed out. There's nothin' for miles but what you see now, trees. No you don't get a cut, fuck you think this is. No you won't fuck clients in here, this is ya'll sleepin quarters." Larry went in his pocket and pulled out slips of paper. "Everybody gets a number, remember it. Someone will take ya'll one by one to get gussied up and have yo pic taken for our customers to see their choices. Once trust is earned and you can move about freely, you'll all meet in the lobby once we open." With a last look my way, Larry knocked twice on tha door, walked out, leavin' us to our thoughts. True to Larry's word, one by one we were called out by our numbers, led down a hall blind folded and into a room where a rack of skimpy gear hung; and a small oval table sat with make-up and mirror, another table held all kinds of heels. I was lucky enough to get number six, so I didn't have to sit twiddlin' my thumbs, I needed a look-see on the layout. So far everythin' had been on tha first floor, so I started countin' tha steps it took to get from A to B. I knew they wouldn't keep us blind folded forever; so if trust was what they needed, I'd serve 'em up a big dose of it. Once I got away, these mafuckas better leave tha U.S. cause all bets were off. * Dove sipped a glass of wine, feeling relaxed in a tub full of hot bubbly water scented with jasmine oils. A soapy foot traveled up her leg. "How you feelin' ma?" Asked Kione who sat at the opposite end. She smiled. "Good bae. Thanks for the bath, it was a nice surprise." cooed Dove, batting her eyes. Kione smiled, "C'mon let's rinse off, your massage awaits." Smiling bright, Dove did as requested; then strode into the hotel room Kione had surprised her with. "Lay down." Kione huskily said, penis standing at attention. Smile bright, Dove stretched out face down then moaned when warm liquid was poured on her back and he slowly massaged; the smell of blueberries teased her nose. "Umm, that feels so good." said Dove, damn near droolin' she was so relaxed. Kione's hands lowered, gently rubbin' and squeezin' cheeks, then slowly lowered to backs of thighs; her legs splayed open offering up a slice of heaven. Kione didn't take the bait, instead he nibbled on her earlobe and whispered, "Turn over." Nipples hard, pussy soaked, Dove rolled over and opened her mouth wide; only for a slice of strawberry to be set on her tongue. 'Okay.' thought

Dove. 'Not what I was expectin', but it's a start.' Kione continued massagin' while slidin' Dove pieces of cantaloupe, watermelon and cherries. "Feelin' better now?" Dove pouted. "A lil." Kione held up an L. "Well lets keeps the party goin'." And they did, ending it with a roundin' romp of toe curlin' sex and then drifted off to sleep. Frownin' at her reflection in tha bathrooms mirror, Dove stuck her tongue out. Kione still slept, so she tried not to let her anger escalate to where she destroyed the hotels bathroom. Things were goin' so good..and then Brian and his bullshit ruined it. Her eyes hardened wit' hate. She knew Tiphanie's ole rotten womb ass put Brian up to havin' her served wit' court papers. They were plannin' on takin' Jeff away from her. Why couldn't mafuckas leave her be? Her hands unconsciously squeezed the towel rack she'd been unaware of holdin' until she snatched it from the wall. The towel slid to the floor as Dove raised it to bash the mirror, then remembered Kione was in the bed. A small grin formed, Kione. Her smile widened becomin' more sadistic. Yess, Kione. So desperate, so eager to please.

CHAPTER FOUR

"You!" Yelled one of the guards who still hid their identity behind masks. He then pointed at Hannah, "Come with me." Hannah nervously glanced around tha room, panic shinin' from her eyes. "Now!" He ordered. Skittish, heart poundin', Hannah sped across tha room and was quickly ushered out. "What was that about?" Linda asked. "Who cares." grunted Sharon, turnin' her hand this way and that as she painted her fingernails. Ump! Honestly, I'm glad Snow White got booted; 'cause she was on my last damn nerve, okay. Twenty-four seven her ass acted like she lived in a cave and ain't know shit 'bout tha world. I'm like, cut it out boo; cause every night you and Sophie bed hoppin', bumpin' and eatin' each other's pus' like we don't hear ya moanin' and meowin' when you buss a fat one, okay. Yo ass probably done slobbed on and rode more dicks then me okay, I'm just sayin'.

Chatter was goin' back and forth when tha door opened and some heavy set mixed breed hoe wearin' a nightgown was shoved in tha room. Ole gurl looked like they kicked her ass real good, ya heard. She was willie lumped tha fuck up! Between tha bruises, tears and snot, I couldn't tell how she normally looked. "Damn gurl, who beat cho ass?!" I asked. Shit, maybe she ain't see it comin'. Yeah right. Chuckle. "Oh Lord, another crier." lamented Sharon with an eyeroll. Linda, havin' pity on snotty lump lump, helped her up and walked her over to Hannah's bed. Usin' lumpy's sleeve, Linda wiped her eyes and nose; and felt bad for whoever she was. A black and blue knot rested on her forehead, another covered her left cheek and one eye was swollen shut; even her lips were discolored. "It's okay, pull yourself together. You don't want them to hear you and they come back in here." Those words worked, 'cause she quickly cut that shit short. Thank God, 'cause a headache was loomin'. "You're right, thank you." a soft, wavery voice said. Linda patted her back, "What's your name?" she asked. "Tiphanie." Oh shit! My eyes widened. Ain't to many chicks stridin' round wit' tha name Tiphanie. I never got a look at her, but I knew she and Dove's brother/baby daddy were a couple. Ump, chile Dove's ass done flipped tha fuck out. A light clicked on. Dove! Ooo dat loony tunes behind all dis shit! That's why her ass wasn't home when Glenda and I got to her place. Tha shit was staged, she knew if we hadn't seen nor heard from her sooner or later we'd swing by. Anger raced through me. Dat jealous, hatin', back stabbin', loose pussy hoe! She ain't have half a brain to put dis into affect. So who was helpin' her besides Larry and Reba? I sneered, cause those two were non fuckin' factors. Dozens of possibilities came and went, 'cause not too many niggas stick around after taggin' Dove's wide load. Trust and believe, Taylor Janae James will figure it out; and God help 'em when I do. Grand opening had arrived. Dove made sure word got out about the opening and was ready to get shit poppin'. All the girls had a spin and knew what was what; and the punishment dealt out if they didn't comply. Dove smiled. Ole Taylor hadn't been a problem like she'd thought she'd be. She'd so looked forward to torturing her ass if she didn't do as told; but once again like a cat, the bitch landed on her feet. Dove lit up a cigarette contemplating her next move now that Tiphanie had joined the Dark Cavern stable. Just thinkin' about how she snatched Tiphanie got her pussy to jumpin'. Dove, Larry and Kione had cased out Brian and Tiphanie's house for three days, then made their move. Brian had enrolled Jeff in a daycare called Babies Like Us until his birthday when he'd attend Jamoke's pre-k class. That pissed Dove off. 'How dare that barren bitch decide to put her son in daycare without askin' her input?' thought Dove. Brian had left for work, which angered her even more. 'Brian hadn't worked a day when we were together.' she stewed. The group waited an additional five minutes to make sure Brian didn't double back. Once the coast was clear, Dove told Larry and Kione to stand on the side of the house and once the door was open she'd signal them to join her inside. The plan worked beautifully. Upon seein' her knockin' through a curtain hung over the doors window, Tiphanie rolled her eyes, then yanked the door open; only to be shoved so hard she tripped over a garbage bag and fell on her ass. Larry and Kione fell in step behind her, then closed and locked the door. "Hi Tip', how's it goin'?" Dove had asked, even though her answer didn't matter. Stunned, eyes wide, Tiphanie stared between the three, pupils full of questions. "Stand up, we're gonna take a lil ride." Tiphanie's head rapidly shook in the negative. "No! Leave my house right this instant or I'll call the police!" Tiphanie had yelled in outrage. Dove gave a deep laugh. "Nah, you won't be callin' anyone. Boys, help ole Tiphanie up." Mouth open to scream, it was quickly shoved back down her throat when Larry tightly slapped his hand over it. Tiphanie bit the fleshy part of Larry's thumb, then prayed her jaw wasn't dislocated or worse; broken when a fist crashed into it. Her head smacked linoleum as both Kione and Larry rained punches everywhere. The last thing she saw before slippin' into dream land was Dove advancing, unfurling rope she pulled from her purse. Dove tweaked hardened nipples as she recalled Tiphanie's beatin' followed by Larry and Kione havin' a turn between cellulite thighs; her cell set on record catching every second. "Can I help you with that?" jarred Dove from thoughts of Tiphanie's kidnap, beating and rape. Hex, fresh from the shower, towel wrapped around his waist, beads of water cascadin' down muscular chest; had Dove comin' out of clothes lickety split. She sunk to her knees, yanked towel away and gently cupped Hex's sac. No more masks was my first thought when tha door swung open; and my damn mouth slid open when YoYo's jailbird ass strode all cocky like in tha room. Well I'll be a monkey's fuckin' uncle. YoYo and Reba were down wit' dis mess. Ooo I can't wait to take it to these he-she's! Okay, I mean buss they shit to tha white meat, red gravy baby! Seein' these two reassured me that I was dead on the money when I said Dove was behind alla this. I still hadn't seen Glenda who I hoped was alright 'cause Glenda had done nothin' but try to be dis loony bitches friend. Ump, some tricks just neva learn. They always twist shit to suit their wants and needs and have a fuckin' fit when shit doesn't go their way; ruinin' true friendships, fuckin' yo man behind yo back while smilin' in yo face, just skraight up triflin'. This hoe can never be me, no matter how bad she wants it. Why? 'Cause I keep shit real boo, I tell it like it mafuckin' is okay; and I don't give a hoot who don't like it, cause it's a free gotdamn country, just faker than a four dollar bill. I'm just sayin'. "Let's go." broke me from my thoughts. The six of us stood and followed behind them; gotta turn to pussy cause tha dick don't want cha ass bitches. I'll say one thing, walkin' around without a damn blindfold feels gooder then a mug. My eyes were bouncin' all over tha place. An emergency exit we passed was chained and padlocked, there were no windows, just a bunch of closed doors. Turnin' tha corner, my eyes widened. Thick black and grey carpet, cream colored alligator leather side tables, two chaise lounges and Italian lacquered baroque sofas. ump, Dove's ass ain't do this, her ass left her apartment lookin' like she was related to Billy goats, I'm just sayin'. Okay, 'cause any and errbody knows if yo bra and panties don't match and smell like Munster, yo apartment is definitely nasty boo okay. Anyhoo, on tha walls were big colored pictures of each girl dressed and lookin' fly; layin, sittin' wit' legs splayed. Eyes scannin' fo' Glenda's picture was halted as six more girls entered tha room and there she was. Glenda smiled, gave a nod and mouthed what looked like 'Dove'. Smirk. I know boo, and when I see dat tramp they betta have my ass chained and surrounded, cause it's on! "A'ight, show time ladies. Remember yo number, 'cause when it's called you'll go down the opposite hall and use tha room that corresponds with yo number." Barked Reba's ole pussy lickin' behind. In walked a bunch of men. Ump a gotdamn smorgasbord; tall, short, thin, hefty, black, white, Hispanic and more. When they saw us positioned around tha room, eyes lit up and chops were licked in anticipation. Girls were bein' picked left and right, but we had no way of knowin' who picked us 'cause they were told to pick tha number attached to tha bottom of tha frame. "Number six." Aww shit, here we go, Standin', I strode towards tha hall, frownin; when YoYo fell in step behind me. Damn hoe, I don't need a fuckin' babysitter, just to walk a hall fulla numbered doors okay. Yo ass must wanna watch; ole nasty, crunchy boxers bitch. Too bad I don't got a broomstick to make you feel at home, I'm just sayin'. Room six was filled wit' everythin' a hoe needs to please tha custie; shit like eatable underwear, fruits, whipped cream and whatnot. A glass cabinet stood against tha wall that held whips, chains, cuffs, anal beads and such; and was locked wit' a padlock. Tha door opened, haltin' my perusal. Some tall, reed thin, hick complete wit' cowboy boots and hat sauntered in like his ass was home range bound, 'bout to fry up a freshly caught deer or some shit. "Howdy lil lady. My my you sure are a pretty filly." Tha fuck is a filly? Country boy gone get a chop to tha throat if dats slang for nigga. "Hmm, well hello stranger. What's yo pleasure this evenin'?" Gag. He smiled, revealin' three of his bottom choppers were missin'. Maybe that filly knocked them joints out, I'm just sayin'. "Aww shucks ma'am, well, to be honest this is my first time in this type of establishment. Plus I've never laid wit' a colored female before, so I'm kinda nervous. Maybe you can take the reins on this one." Chile, I ain't understand half tha shit country boy said, my ass still tryina decipher what tha hell a filly is okay. They should have a 'how to understand country boys' for dummies up in here boo, okay. Smile wide, I crossed tha room. Stoppin' right in front of him, I ran a hand from tha top button on his shirt to his belt buckle, which by tha way was big as hell and had a pic of horse and rider on it. "First timer eh? A'ight, just relax and let dis filly fulfill all yo desires." "Uhm, okay. My names Billy Ray by the way." Yawn. Ninja I don't give a good gotdamn what cho name is, unless its first name: Will Help last: You Escape okay boo. So don't tell me yo life story, 'cause yo ass will put me in a damn coma. Billy Bob, Billy Goat, what tha hell never nodded, then swallowed. His Adams apple bobbed all kinds of crazy in a chicken neck he called a throat. Unbuttonin' his flannel shirt brought into view a patch of hair on a ribs and protrudin' chest; and when pants and boxers dropped, good googily moogily. Dis ninja was scrawny as hell! Just extra damn bony. I know when he walked and dem bones shook and rattled he looked and sounded crazy. Ump, so damn skinny his nipples touch; so skinny ass and balls look like one item; so skinny he looks like a mic stand, I'm just sayin'. Seven curved inches was surrounded by patches of pubic hair. Da fuck ninja, you got alopecia of tha balls? I'd already swiped a condom, so I tore it open, placed it in my mouth and sucked him in. "Sshit!" squealed out as his toes balled up in knots. Well damn boo, I ain't even get started yet and yo ass already 'bout to blow. Smirk, cause dats what happens when you come to tha best boo okay, you get hooked a'ight. You start missin' work so you can be first in line when tha doors open; eyes peeled lookin' fo' me okay. I'm just sayin'. "Cats whiskers, please don't stop!" He pleadingly yelled, hips pistonin'. Breathe okay, cause CPR is extra ninja. Something thumped on tha floor. Gazin' downward, I see ole Billy Bob's cell done fell out his pocket. Alright now! Easin' up a lil, 'cause now I don't want his ass comin' jack rabbit quick. I reached down, flipped it open and didn't see a lock code. Damn what's Ty's number? Or Omaire for that matter? Fuckin' A B and C! Think Tay', think! All I could remember of Omaire's number was the first three and the last four of Ty's. Ooo, I could beat my own ass right now! Flippin' tha phone closed, I took care of Billy Jean, then got ready for tha next customer. Six custies later I was mad as fuck. I'm like how I'm a hoe in a hoe house givin' up tha pus' fo' free and not nan one got me off or had a fuckin' cell that wasn't locked. Kinda shit is that!? It's like havin' fifty cents to use a payphone and not ones in sight cause SNET (Southern New England Telephone) done pulled 'em all up. Not everybody has a cell phone okay and even if they do, half tha time yo joints off cause you ain't pay tha bill. It's like yo rag startin' and ain't a pad or tampon in sight, I'm just sayin'. Anyhoo, I did clip a few dollars from each custie though. Twenty from Billy Goat, the last outta some dude who said his name was Jones; cheap bastard only had five bucks. Anotha had nothin' but lint; wallet so dry moths flew out, I'm just sayin'. I stuck it inside tha kitty kat bank in case they wanna strip search a bitch. Surprisingly we all were allowed to shower before bein' escorted back to our prison. The next day, peppermint breath came and drug Tiphanie kickin' and screamin' from tha room. "Sup wit' that?" Rochelle asked; which shocked me 'cause I thought tha hoe was mute or somethin'. "What?" asked Sharon, eyin' Rochelle all hard. "Why they take ole girl? She came back later then us and now she's out before breakfast's even served. Let me find out she's the favorite, she'll start snitchin' on all of us." A few brows arched at Rochelle's words. "Nah it ain't that." threw out Linda, "Last night before they came for us, she started tellin' me that some chick name Dove beat her up and took her from her home. Said dis Dove chicks gotta buncha loose screw that she's angry and bitter cause her baby daddy took her kid and wants nothin' to do wit' her." Yeah, yeah, tell it to tha choir. Betta yet, tell me somethin' I don't fuckin' know, okay boo. If you gone spread tha news at least get somethin' I ain't heard or figured out my damn self, I'm just sayin'. No one said a word, I guess to let her words marinate. Anyhoo lunch of hotdogs, French fries and grape Kool-Aid that tasted like it ain't have a drop of sugar came in. I'm sayin', Kool-Aid's a hood staple okay. How you gone make some and leave out tha damn sugar? That's like yo pus' fallin' off and you still tryin to fuck. It's like wantin' yo dick sucked but no one will touch it cause its fulla big ass pus bumps, okay. Disgusted, I left that shit and just ate tha lunch that was in-between lukewarm and cold. Chatter between tha girls went back and forth, which I pretty much ignored til talk turned to tha guards. "I heard that afro wearin' dyke lookin' chicks pretty dangerous." said one. Another sucked her choppers and spat, "I heard she's been in and out of jail a rack of times." "So fuckin' what!" snapped Rochelle. "People go to jail every damn day, that shit means nothin'." "True. said Sharon, joinin' in. "I found out that Reba chicks really a dude." Jaws hung open at her words. "Oh yeah, how you figure?" I asked. Fuck it, I joined in; ain't like I got shit else to do. "The other day when she walked me to the bathroom, I lied and said there wasn't no toilet paper. So when she got some and handed it over, I accidently ran my hand over crotch and was about to offer a pussy lick when I ain't feel no pussy. In other words, Reba ain't no damn chick, she's a dude." "No way!" "Get outta here!" "You lie!" Were all tossed out when Sharon shared that juicy tidbit of news. Ump, yes boo. Ron, Reba, whateva tha fuck she's callin' herself this month was definitely not a male; 'cause dick wasn't swingin' between her thighs unless she had on a strap on, I'm just sayin'. Tha door swung open and Tiphanie's shoved back in tha room. All talk ceased 'cause ole Tiphanie looked zoned tha hell out. Before I knew it, I'd crossed tha room and stood before Tiphanie. Her head bobbed around on her neck, along wit' eyes that continually rolled in their sockets. "Tip." I smacked her ass. "Focus. What happened?" "Hunh?" A lil drool ran from lip to chin. Gross ass. I gave a lil shake. "What'd they do to you Tip'?" I asked again cause a bitch needed to know if they planned on doin' to me what they'd done to her ass. Fuck everyone else, this was all about self preservation ya heard. "I..uh.." her voice faded out and tha head bob started back up. Linda burst out laughin'. "Fuck so funny?" Snarled Rochelle, chile all this cattiness was givin' my ass a headache, okay. "The bitch is high; most likely heroin. Trust, I know the signs when I see 'em." Aww shit, ugly girls right. Bitch so ugly her name should be 'shit happens'. She so ugly her Doctor is a vet, I'm just sayin'. Damn, her ugly ass got me off track. What was I sayin'? Oh yeah, Tiphanie was higher than a kite. Snatchin' both arms I gave 'em a look-see and sure 'nough, a needle prick lay in crook of her arm. Damn, Dove has truly gone too damn far okay; just totally done lost it boo, skraight coo cook for coco puffs. I'm sayin', has this chick always been crazy and just hid it when around my ass? I swear I ignored all signs, figurin' Dove was just jealous when all along tha hoe was plottin' and schemin'. Fuck!

CHAPTER FIVE

Fuckin' A! I've been here seven months! Damn, times flyin' okay; somethin's gotta give. A bitch needs a sign, some damn thang before I snap okay; 'cause these bitches, these custies is makin' me insane. The door opened and in walked peppermint breath. Dude ain't talk much which annoyed me, 'cause I had questions that needed fuckin' answers; but dis nucca would just give a blank stare like he was on another fuckin' planet, okay. Hell, I even tried to give him some a dese good ass snacks and dude's pecker wouldn't rise to tha occasion. Ole dead dick bastard! Ooo I'm goin' crazy up in here, so I pulled Sharon to tha side and whispered was she down to jump Reba and YoYo; take any keys they had and rise tha hell up outta here. Ole girl was down, so we bided our time; and when Larry surprised us wit' a visit we pounced on his lil ass. Nigga so short his besties an ant, I'm just sayin'. I went high, Sharon went low.

Larry's head hit tha metal bed frame hard as hell, then lay still. Frozen, Sharon and I stared at each other then back at Larry whose head was leakin' blood; one a dem bitches screamed. I swear if I don't make it out, I'mma take it to her fuckin' face! Sharon quickly patted Larry's pockets, came out wit' two sets of keys. "Let's go! You dumb bitches can go or stay, makes me no neva mind." I snarled, jumped to my feet and ran to tha door, Sharon on my heels. Yankin' open tha door, I peeked out, saw an empty hall; took a breath and went for it. Speed walkin' down tha hall, I mentally counted steps; turned left at twenty-five and there was tha chained padlocked door callin' us from the end of tha hall. "Oh shit, there's the door. I can smell freedom bitch, we're gonna make it." panted Sharon, hope shinin' bright in her eyes. "Stop!" Boomed a voice. Best believe I took tha hell off, Sharon on my heels when a loud bang rang out. Sharon hit tha floor and skidded. Clippin' my heel, I joined her on tha floor; arms length away from escapin'. 'Get up Taylor, move yo ass!' My conscious screamed. Knees throbbin', I crawled; iggin' tha voice behind me yellin' to "Get down or get shot." Gone head boo, cause picture me willingly layin' down and givin' up. His ass must be smokin' some hella ganja, cause he's trippin' okay. Still on my knees shit seemed to hit slow mo. I jammed a key from tha ring that held five keys in the lock, but it didn't turn; neither did tha second. "C'mon mafucka, c'mon!" I yelled, heart poundin' sweat beadin' forehead. "Taylor! Stop or I'll shoot!" I could hear him chamber a round, but I wouldn't stop. I wouldn't quit and lay down. A female yelled, "No! Taze her don't shoot, I want her alive!" I jammed a key in from the second set, twisted it and tha lock popped open. I knew I didn't have enough time to unravel tha chain, but I gave it tha ole college try. I screamed, hit tha floor and felt my whole body tense up. I swear I even felt my toes curl in tha opposite direction from tha shock of what felt like 50,000 volts surgin' through me. Dazed, frozen in place, tha charge ended, releasin' tha stranglehold it had upon me. A trickle of urine eased out followed by a steady stream as heels clicked nearer until stoppin' right beside my hip. Blurry eyes traveled past Max Azria heels, up slightly hairy legs, to a peach Fendi figure huggin' dress; a neck wit' a Leviev choker and finally to a face I knew well, my last thought right before that Azria kicked me in tha face was, 'Damn, business was good, cause this skank had a complete make-over.' "Oww." I whined, comin' to, Chile my body hurt! Felt like I let a beached whale chill atop me for hours okay. Raisin' an arm to rub sleep crusted eyes, I was immediately halted before my arm got half way. My eyes flew open. Both arms were tied down wit' what appeared to be torn pieces of sheet at tha wrist. I lifted my head and my feet were as well, leavin' 'em spread eagled. My eyes bounced around tha room haltin' at tha sight of a thick ass belt, a wooden paddle, what looked like nipple clamps, whips, handcuffs, gags and more. Aww fuck no! Now I like freaky kinky sex as much as tha next chick, but dis shit here was too much okay. Nipple clamps? Seriously, my nipples ached just seein' dat shit a'ight. A bitch started struggilin' cause I ain't down wit' tha get down. Hell yeah I like to be spanked, who doesn't, but whippin' my ass til I can't sit down cause my ass bleedin' and not cause tha sex got a lil rough, is out! Ahh, I pass. I wear enough of those when I visit jail cause I've beat a hoe down and she's mad so tha boys in blue are called. Sometimes if my boy Orlando was workin' he'd take me out tha cell and back to his office where he'd order Chinese, then we'd fuck all over his office. Too bad his wife caught us. To appease her ole insecure ass, captain Orlando Higgins packed up his home, wife of ten years, his two sons, their cat and moved to L.A. I could sure use his help right now. I'm just sayin'. Sputterin', chokin' from ice cold water thrown in my face, I glared at a smug Dove holdin' an empty water container. I must've fell asleep or dis hoe changed clothes every couple hours, 'cause now she wore a fatigue cami top, skin tight dark green For All Mankind jeans and some cute Walter Steiger boots, while her hair was snatched to tha side in a slicked down ponytail. Her face was perfectly made up so damn good, I felt like a hag lyin' trussed up, compared to her and I ain't neva, eva eva, fell or felt second place when it came to Dove's nasty ass, I'm just sayin'.

"Damn Tay' you look a hot ass mess girlfriend, I'm just sayin'." she mocked. "A'ight I'll let you have that one cause it's obvious you wanna be me." I laughed. "Too bad it'll never happen, no matter how hard you fake it. Know why? 'Cause I'm classy boo. I don't walk around in mis matched panty and bras. I don't wear safety pins okay and I for damn sure don't strut around wit' a pus' so loose it's a wonder tha shit ain't fall on tha floor. Nor does my snatch stink, burn, itch or ooze okay; so alla dem clothes and made up face don't mean squat when beneath it you're still tha same ole nasty slut bucket you've always been." Bam! I cheesed, dat hoe was heated. If looks could kill, I'd be somewhere roastin' on a pit drenched in bbq sauce. Dove's teeth ground together while her hands squeezed tha container so hard every vein from forearms to finger tip bulged. "Go head and attack me while I'm tied down like tha snake you are." "Shut up!" Screamed Dove, eyes wild. "You think you know me, but you don't! You don't know what I've been through and why I am tha way I am! All you care about is Taylor. You're fake, a fake friend. This is where fake bitches like you end up. No one cares enough about you to even know you're gone; they've got peace and quiet hoe. So don't come for me boo cause you won't like my answers." My smile widened 'cause I was underneath that bitch skin like a tick burrowin' fo' blood. "Ooo, if I wasn't tied down I'd be shakin' in fear." Lies! Tha only thing I felt was rage and if I got off dis bed I'd rip her fuckin' empty ass head clean off. Shocked, no words slid pass them dick suckers, I jeered, "So what's tha plan genius, or did you not think that far ahead? Matter fact, I know yo ass definitely ain't tha brains of this operation, so who and where's our mystery guest?" Dove nervously fingered tha container refusin' to meet my pryin' eyes. Ump, I done hit tha ding bat in tha knee caps. Ole Dovey Dove had a partner and as sure as dis snapper between spread thighs can reel in a big fish, I can still read dis hoe like a Linette King book. Ooo chile, dat chick right there write tha fire ya heard! "D..don't worry a.. about if I have a p..partner or not." she stammered. Pitiful, just f'n pitiful. "Well since your holdin' that container, put it to good use and come catch dis pee I gotta let fly." Yeah I'm lyin', but she ain't know dat. All kinds of emotions slid across her face, shock that I'd asked her that. Hmm, was that a hint of desire I saw flicker behind extended lashes? "It won't bite." I purred, "I can see it all ova yo face that you wanna taste me." my voice lowered, became husky. "Do you remember how I taste, how sweet it was on yo tongue?" I threw in a moan. "It felt so good, no one can do me like you boo." Dove's breathin' escalated. "Tha way yo tongue swept out; teasin', lickin', suckin'. Mmm I miss it Dove, I miss you." I need an Academy Award okay. I'm just sayin', cause right now I got her right where I want her. Another moan, a lil wind of hip, a lick of lips and I felt tha bed dip. Gotcha! A finger slowly trailed up my calf. Dove's head lowered, she inhaled, her nose restin' on mound. "Yess." hissed out. "Please me Dove, as only you can. I fantasize about you Dove, I really do, all tha time." Her tongue sensuously swept out, slowly, gently tastin' dis goodness right before she started feastin'. "Sss, mmm, yess. Boo eat it, eat it!" Yeah okay, okay tha shit was feelin' good so why not enjoy it while playin' wit' Dove's mind? Tongue stiffened, she poked and prodded; sucked my clit, blew, hummed, parted cheeks and got her eat on! "Uh, uh, uh." I chanted; undulatin' hips, matchin' every move she made. "Yess boo I..I'm cuminn!" I roared out from an orgasm so powerful my legs shook so hard I caught a damn cramp. Risin', Dove slowly untied my legs, then one arm before bendin' and layin' a deep tongue kiss on me. "Your right." she whispered, starin' all intensely at a bitch. "About everythin'. I wanna say somethin'; don't answer now, just think about it okay." Before I could blink she continued. "I luv you Tay', I always have. I admire you so much. It's true that I try and emulate everythin' you do, which is why I do and say what I do and say." Say what now? Luv. Dis trick done really gone off tha damn deep end a'ight. "I want us to be together, you and me." Well ain't that what together usually means, I'm just sayin'. "We can rule and run this together Tay', full partners. No more locked doors, you can come and go as you please." Dove walked to tha door, opened it and said. "Think about it, m'kay." blew a kiss and walked out. Back in my room, I still couldn't believe all that Dove had said. Sharon was nowhere to be found and tha girls were annoyin' tha hell outta me to tha point where I asked to be moved to another room. I ended up wit' Donell who I was shocked to see and a dude named Barry. Come to find out, Donell was there of his own free will, tha fucks that about?! Then I remembered Donell sold ass/pussy to make a way. Tha other one, named Barry aka Belinda, made Donell look like a drag queen huntie; where Donell was stocky and hairy. Ole Belinda actually had curves and was hair free cause I ain't need to be 'round a room full a wolves sheddin' every damn where okay. Anyhoo, Belinda either had good genes or a fantastic stylist cause tha bitch's hair was slayed a'ight. Shoulder length thick, reddish black locks that seemed to sway and bounce from a summer breeze when ain't no type a breeze blowin'. Thick loose curls hung along wit' a side bang. Her face wasn't made up, but seemed to glow as if it were; perfectly plucked brows, thin nose and full lips, my eyes dropped to one a them sports bras that was full of 36B cup breasts, a flat washboard belly. Ump, I knew tha cat fights between tha two would be poppin' off, 'cause jealousy had to be chewin' at his innards, I'm just sayin'. "Tay'!" Squealed Donell runnin' up and givin' me a hug. Hol' up! Wait a ball garglin' diggity damn sec! Since when did me and Donell chill enough to be huggin' a bitch hunh? And all dat damn squealin' like we besties who ain't seen each other since birth. See, dis what pisses me off, don't be all extra boo okay. I see you, hell everybody can hear yo loud ass voice, voice so high sounds like bed springs squeakin'. Shit so high he makes Alvin and The Chipmunks sound like Michael Clarke Duncan, I'm just sayin'. "Hey gurl, whatchu doin' here?" I asked. Belinda coughed, muttered, "Not makin' any money, that's for damn sure." kinda under her breath, but loud enough to be heard. Donell smacked her lips, "Anyway, cause I'm talkin' to Tay', not no damn wannabe." Ooo hackles raisin', I can use a lil excitement okay. I mean, they wanna be called she, so are they gonna scratch and windmill, throw a few slaps or let tha man in 'em come out and throw some break yo face punches? I'm curious okay. Ignorin' his question, I asked him one. "Girl why you call Belinda a wannabe? I thought you people band together." Yeah I said it, like I said before, a bitch needs some entertainment a'ight. "Cause he,...." Donell stressed tha latter, "wants to be a bitch. He wants to be me gurl. When he came up in here lookin' like a worn out dish rag, I showed him the ropes. I upgraded the make-up girl, cause his ass was wearin' a shade two shades lighter okay. I'm the one who showed him all the trade tricks and secrets and now he's got a lil fame up here; done got the big head, if that's even possible, and now he thinks he's the queen bee up in here! Tay' you betta tell dis hooker who I am and what I'm 'bout befo' its anotha dead bitch up in The Dark Cavern!" Donell yelled all hype and shit. Aww sukey now, ding ding, round one. Then I realized what Donell had said, dead bitch. Who and what did I miss while tied to tha bed getting' tha pus' ate. "Wait, pause and rewind. Who's dead?" A sinkin' feelin' assailed me. "Some tall bitch from room three, I don't know nor care what her name was. She and some other trick were tryin to escape. Joe's ole trigger happy ass capped her in tha back and was 'bout to shoot tha otha, luckily Dove showed up and stopped Joe's ass from killin' her too. She ended up getting' tased." My back still itched where tha taser's two prongs had hit, shockin' and drawin' tiny beads of blood. I now sported two scabs. "Ump girl, you always come wit' tha news." "Damn right I do. Hmp, and til otha bitches respect tha queen, they'll stay getting' plugged while I sit back reapin' tha benefits." Belinda jumped up. "I'm tired of yo ass tellin' any and everyone who'll listen that you saved me, or upgraded me. So what, what chu want a gay award of the year cause you showed me a few tricks?" Belinda jeered. "I've thanked you, but damn, if you're waitin' for me to kiss yo feet and lick yo ass you'll be waitin' a hella long time!" "Xcuse me Tay', let me handle dis trash right quick." said Donell. Ump, bitches is just messy. They always startin' shit, or feedin' tha fire. Can't we all just get along? I'm just sayin'. Donell got within kissin' distance and spat, "Hoe please, ain't nothin' here but space and mafuckin' opportunity. Don't talk 'bout it, be 'bout it; cause you gotta mouth." then mushed Belinda so hard in tha forehead she had no choice but to take a step back, or end up fallin' to tha floor. "Stupid cunt!" "Yo stankin' ass momma!" Returned Donell, accompanied by punch to Belinda's eye. "Argh! You ugly man bitch!" Shrieked Belinda, servin' Donell wit' two quick jabs to the face and body. Takin' a seat on tha bed, I peeped a soft pack of Salem 100's atop tha pillow wit' a small purple fifty cent Bic lighter. These two were goin' at it, so I shook one free, lit up and got my puff on; and watched tha show. It ended wit' a cheap shot to balls by Donell. Belinda crumpled, got stomped a few times which bounced her head off tha floor a few times. "Stupid bitch, tricks are for washed up trades like you; tryin' a make a comeback." Taunted Donell before hawkin' up a wad of spit, lettin' it fly where it landed on a moanin' Belinda's forehead. "Guess you're outta commission fo' tha night."

CHAPTER SIX

Ump, for a week I dragged on my answer to Dove's partnership plans. Momma ain't raise no fool, so you already know my answers gonna be yes. I just wanted to see how bad her ass wanted it. I'm like a cat cornerin' a mouse boo; I'll swat it, and watch it while hungrily lickin' lips. I might even let it run a few paces before re-catchin' it. It's all 'bout tha mind games boo and Taylor's a master manipulator okay. Anyhoo, durin' that time I was client free; which had Donell and Belinda feelin' some type of way; like I gave a fuck how they felt, a'ight. I'm just sayin', if I wanted to roam tha halls all I had to do was knock twice. I even got to sit in tha backyard, even though murderin' ass Joe was wit' me tha whole time. While everybody else ate simple shit like burgers and hotdogs, yo gurl was munchin' on skrimps and crab legs. Fuck Kool-Aid; Pepsi, wine coolers, anythin' I asked for, best believe I got it. So I decided I needed to see Glenda. Reba escorted me wit' a bunch of under her breath mutterin' See, that's tha shit I'm talkin' 'bout. Be a man 'bout yours boo, okay. Since you struttin' round dis piece like yo imaginary balls hang low, shim please, ain't nobody studyin' or worried 'bout cho bound breasts okay. Poof, be gone okay. I know shim's feelin' some type 'cause it's got a thing for Dove, which ain't got a squirrels balls to do wit' me okay. Don't be J boo, this what I do in my mafuckin' sleep, okay. Tha fans boo, it's all 'bout tha fans. When you grow up and get chu some, come back we'll talk, I'm just sayin'. "I'll be back in an hour." growled ole tight lips. I started to say somethin', but why give her what she fiened for. Instead, I served Reba's ass a big bowl of ignore, get out my face, walked in room three and smiled when I spotted Glenda sewin' in a weave on some light bright bald headed trick. Ump, lip smack. Invest in some Mane n Tail, some Dax hair grease boo; 'cause them edges are strugglin'. I'm just sayin', cause errbody can't have long hair, but that uneven mess atop her melon needs some serious help, stat! "Oh my god, Tay'!" Screamed Glenda as she jumped up and ran over, greetin' me wit' hug and kiss. "Jeez girl, enough already. Back up off me." Glenda giggled but I'm serious as hell okay, I'm just sayin'. "Are you okay? Are you comin' in here? We've got two empty beds. I heard Dove's behind this bullshit, I can't believe she would do this to us." she rattled off in one breath. "Whoa girlie, slow down and breathe. You know I charge fo' performin'

CPR." Glenda laughed like I'd told tha funniest joke she'd ever heard. What. The. Fuck. Ever. "Yes I'm fine, no I'm not bein' moved." although now that she mentioned it, that would be next on my list. "And yes Dove's behind this." her jaw dropped as her eyes filled wit' tears. "I..I didn't wanna believe it Tay'. I thought we were friends; friends don't kidnap friends and make them prostitute at a hoe house." A lone tear rolled down her face, followed by a few sniffs. Sad, puppy dog save tha world eyes stared at me. "What are we gonna do Tay', hunh? I have a life, a son that I wanna get home to, and Marcus. I know he's lookin' for me, he's probably worried sick." Uh no boo. Right before Sharon got popped she'd fucked ole Marcus. She'd come back to tha room braggin' 'bout how Marcus was proposin' once she got through wit' him. Besides that, Glenda's pic was on tha fuckin' wall, so he knew her ass was here. Do you think he said somethin' like, 'Hey that's my missin' girl right there.' or how 'bout, you could've chosen Glenda instead of Sharon so you could've found out from tha horses mouth on why tha love of yo life's locked in a hoe house. Niggas, I swear. That's why I fuck 'em, juice 'em and toss 'em out before they expire; 'cause I don't care 'bout you fallin' in love or wantin' to be exclusive or proposin'. Ninja please okay, I'm just sayin'. "Calm down, I'm sure lil Marvin's fine, and we'll find a way outta here. Just hang in there." "Uh hello! Are you gonna finish my head or talk to that old ass diva all damn day!" Ooo no baldy locks didn't! The switch flipped, fuck jigglin'. "Don't come fo' me boo okay. Grown folks are talkin' right now, that means shut tha hell up and wait okay cause my girls doin' yo fucked up head a favor boo. Thank God cause that uneven shit looks like you ran into a weed wacker a'ight; and make sure you get a bang too boo, cause yo forehead so big it sweat waterfalls. Shit so big I can watch two movies at once." Pow! "Now what hoe!" Glenda burst out laughin' along wit' tha other four girls in tha room. Ole girl jumped up and lost her balance which set off anotha round. "Damn boo slow down, that forehead gotchu all off balance." Laretha who'd been teased all her life about her hair and forehead screamed in rage and charged. Dis chicks screamin', mutterin' and damn near foamin' at tha mouth as she charged like a rabid bull. Just as she ran up I clipped her ass and used her momentum to send her mountain of a forehead right into tha door. "Dammn!" Tha girls yelled out, then burst out laughin' and rankin'. Arms crossed, foot tappin', I waited to see how ole girl wanted to play it. Oh, she wouldn't be playin' or finishin' up her weave. "Good nite hoe." Walkin' back over to tha bed, Glenda was workin' from, I copped a seat and smiled. "How ya'll doin'?" A short, kinda chubby Hispanic chick wit' a mouthful of gold chimed. "Shit, afta seein' that, I ain't got no complaints girlfriend." and smiled. "No worries, unless you come for me nah mean?" She nodded. "I feel you, names Melissa and you are?" "I'm Taylor boo, nice to meet cha." the other girls quickly shared theirs as well, Abby, Denise, Sally and Terri. I chilled for my allowed hour, then was led back to Donell and Belinda's room. "Have you made a decision Tay'?" I could tell Dove was nervous by tha way her eyes bounced around and she fiddled wit' tha polish on her thumb nail. Withholdin' a smirk, I inhaled fresh air as Dove had me escorted outside for privacy. Ohh tha mind games we play.. "I..I've done a lot of thinkin' about us and I..I..." forced tears fell. but what I really wanted to do was a bust a gut laugh okay, cause her ass was truly pathetic. Gee willikers, get cho life boo, damn. Dove gently smiled, then wiped my tears which was all warm, fuzzy and sweet til ha nasty slut bucket sucked my tears from her fingers. "And," she sang eyes all bright and shit. Ugh! I'm just sayin'. "I'm willin' to give us a try, but I'd like to take things slow, if that's okay." eyes lowered demurely. Demurely, ha! I continued wit', "You really hurt me Dove. I wanna trust you, but I'm afraid." And the nominee for best actress in a shitty situation goes to.... Dove leaned in and rained soft, wet kisses from eye to chin, grossin' me tha fuck out. Can you say skin crawlin', cause that's just what tha fucks goin' on okay. I'm just sayin'. "Mmm that feels nice." huskily slid out. Gag me somebody, please. "I love you Tay'." Yeah yeah, you've told me like a hundred times already, jeez.

"And you've made me so happy by agreein' to be wit' me, and of course we can take things slow. I'd do anythin' to earn your trust back." she purred softly, pecked my lips and said, "C'mon I wanna show you somethin'." With a nod of acquiescence, I clasped her ole moist palm in mines and let her lead tha way back inside. At the opposite end of tha hall, YoYo was escortin' some bedraggled creature towards tha showers. "Good Lord, who is that?" Damn right my nosy ass asked. Dove giggled, stopped at a locked door, pulled out a set of keys and replied, "That's Tiphanie's ass." My jaw surely hit tha floor as Dove unlocked and swung tha door open. "C'mon in." she gestured like she was a game show host offerin' up a trip to Cancun. "Tiphanie?! That was Tiphanie? Fuck happened to her?" I asked, followin' her into an office fully decorated wit' all tha trappins; plush wall to wall carpet, lush plants, comfy couch and chairs; she even had a bar set up in tha corner. Takin' a seat on tha couch, I continued my grillin' session 'cause I needed to know just how far up tha crazy ladder her ass had climbed. "Word. What happened, she looks like shit on a stick?" A big ass smile bloomed on her face, "You really think so? Thanks, thanks a lot. I want dat uppity bitch to suffer." An image of Tiphanie in tha hallway came back crystal clear. Where once kinda hefty, Tiphanie was now pleasantly plump. Where once flowin' long hair lay, now was wacked off in uneven clumps and she seemed out of it. "What'd you do to her?" A dreamy, pleased look came over Dove. "Mmm, more like what haven't I done." She mused. Okayy, yep Dove's ass done reached tha top a'ight and wasn't no comin' back no matter how many pills she swallowed. "Like what?" Pout. "See you don't trust me boo, how're we gonna build a life togetha if you can't tell me one lil thing." I made like I was 'bout to bounce. "No!" Yelled Dove, jumpin' up all fast she beat me to tha door. "You're right, I'm sorry. It's just hard for me to trust. Please, sit down; ask me anythin' and I promise to answer okay." Gotcha! Returnin' to couch I resumed sittin' and repeated my question and hunny chile I wish I hadn't. It's a good thang I've got a cast iron stomach, cause dis crazy hoe went on to tell me how she'd been shootin' Tiphanie up wit' dope. How she'd had Joe, Larry and Reba beat her ass every day. Tha shit went on and on endin' wit' how Dove had personally ripped out finger and toenails wit' a pair of pliers. Ump, ump, ump, and she really thought we were gonna rock as one, uh, how 'bout no you crazy bastard! How 'bout you take a long ride wrapped in a straight jacket boo okay, cause ain't nobody tryin' ride wit' queen crazy a'ight; especially my ass. Hell, if I wanted crazy I would've stayed wit' Brandon and if I wanted mood swings, ding, ding, there's Joshua. Fuck, I can't even label dis chick right here okay, cause ain't no help for tha helpless, I'm just sayin'. But what I will do is play her ass like a pair of drums. Make her ass fall so deep in love she won't see me pull this hoe house right from under them hammer toes of hers, okay; and when I'm done, I'll make damn sure her psycho ass can't come back for revenge.

CHAPTER SEVEN

Ooo chile, I'm lovin' this partner bullshit okay. I still wasn't allowed outside by myself, but other than that, Taylor James was all set. Sure there were drawbacks, like spendin' alone time wit' Dove who always wanted to snuggle, kiss and get her feel on. A bitch was so turned off, she asked why my snatch felt like tha Sahara. Duh, cause I ain't attracted to yo ass, 'cause you disgust me. You should be grateful I don't puke all over you; cause every time I gotta play the 'let's make out' game, I wanna snatch dat whip off tha wall, wrap it round yo scrawny ass neck and choke tha hell out cho ass. I'm just sayin'. Anyhoo, I guess the romance bug nibbled her ass. It probably dropped dead right after; 'cause ole dovey Dove pops up wit' flowers when her ass has known me long enough to know I don't do that corny flower and plant crap. A box of heart shaped candy, now that I like; and a meal consistin' of food from Hot Pots. The hoe even bought me lingerie from

Victoria's Secret. Just to keep her hooked; after we ate and I modeled for her, I stretched across tha sofa, spread my thighs and whispered the two lil words that brought a tear to her eye. "Eat me." I whispered, slidin' hands over breasts; a sneak nipple pinch to wake tha girls and get 'em in tha mood. Salivatin', Dove kneeled, slowly removed thong, then stared in awe at plump mound wit' a thin strip of hair down tha center. "I know I've said it before, but you've got tha prettiest snatch I've ever seen, felt and tasted. When yo cum rains on my tongue, it's like tha sweetest cream." Yeah, yeah, let's move shit along so we can get it over wit'. As if she'd heard me, Dove lowered her head, then slowly kissed and nibbled up and down each thigh before divin' in full throttle. Now I give credit where is due and Dove Mitchell can eat da hell out some pus' okay! Do me right gotdamnit! Yess lawd, hit every nook and cranny! Suck on da pearl! Uh, uh, sss, oh shit! Ooo, where's a dick when you need one, cause dis right here's startin' a fire can't no plastic ding a ling put out okay. I need a long, fat, preferbily curved one so it hits every angle while bangin' my cervix. Ten and a half inches boo. Sss, uhh, I wanna feel it tap my spine. Umm, I..I.. wanna deep throat a'ight and you can't do that wit' no fuckin' twat; and especially not one dat stays oozin' itchin' and havin' visitors of tha legged variety okay. Dis freak parted ass cheeks and got her munch on! Hello! Ooo chile get all up in it! Yess, yess, eat dis cake boo. It's hot and sweet;

and causes all kinds of mafuckas to fall weak. Uhh, fuckk, yes lawd I'm cuminnn! I slept like a newborn slid fresh from tha pussy okay, I'm just sayin'. Ump, lip smack, 'cause Dove did tha damn thang! I think that was some of her best work. Tha shit would've had a weak minded hoe fucked up in tha head, okay; but not Taylor boo. It'll take more than a tongue lashin' on my clit to have me all discombobulated, I'm just sayin'. Anyhoo, after I fingered stink box and she got off, I couldn't shut her ass tha hell up okay. A bitch tryin a catch a few zz's and she's all in my fuckin' ear, "I luv you. I wanna tell you tha reason I am tha way I am."; and huntie I heard it all. From bein' born to a multiple personality momma, to droppin' outta school in tha ninth grade. I had to ask could we finish up her life story in tha mornin' cause good Lord I'd spent enough time witcho ass. Can a bitch breathe, fo' real. Now since I'm free to roam and Dove had slid me all keys except for padlocks, I got my roam on after hittin' up tha kitchen. Fixed a turkey and cheese samich and headed back to Dove's office to snoop through tha two file cabinets and her desk. Leavin' tha kitchen I run into YoYo, her big ass almost made me drop my shit. "Watch it bitch." I snapped, catchin' it just in time. YoYo smirked. "Must be nice to suddenly have so much freedom." Duh, ya think? Truly I miss bein' locked tha hell up, who wouldn't? Yep, I liked bein' blindfolded; stupid ass I swear. "Yep, it sure is. Must be hard havin' neither sex be interested in you." I looked YoYo's ass up then down. "Be careful boo." I told her ass. "I'd hate for your P.O. to hear dat you're workin' at a hoe house, isn't that shit illegal boo?" That hoe turned a bright ass red, makin' them wart like freckles stand out even more. Ump, just ugly hunny. Hit up make overs.com, cause yo face needs immediate assistance okay; I'm just sayin'. "Are you threatenin' me you ex hoe?" Snapped YoYo, eyes narrowed in anger. "Girl please. All dis eye squintin' and swellin' up..oops that's yo regular size; dat shit don't pump no fear this way. So what you've been on lock boo, who hasn't okay; and far as threatenin' you, you can take it how you like, 'cause Taylor don't care either way. Just know a few words in tha right ear and yo ass'll be outta work and behind bars; cause dem Percs you up here sellin' is illegal too." YoYo gulped. "Chill, I'm jokin'. No need for all that. Can I get chu anythin' Tay'? I mean from outside, I'm on my way out for a few." Ass kissers, I tell ya. Hmm, let's see, how 'bout a big ass steak, a bag of snacks, or how 'bout you sneak one a my toys up in here for a few rounds. A bitch needs to release some stress, I'm backed up okay. Nah, I don't trust her ole booty sniffin' ass. I don't care if we did hang a lil bit back in tha day, cause sooner or later a skunks scent will always be noticeable. "Nope. I'm straight; but thanks for askin'." Takin' a bite of samich I flashed YoYo a bunch of chewed up bread, cheese and meat and walked off. Four days later I talked Dove into givin' tha girls a cookout in tha backyard and we had a ball. We had tha usual food and drinks; afterwards she closed tha Dark Cavern and gave everyone tha night off, which shocked tha shit outta me. Couldn't be me, I'm just sayin'. YoYo was bein' all nice and gag me sweet every time she saw my ass, which had the switch jigglin' cause she's annoyin' tha hell outta me, okay. Her nosy ass caught me goin' through Dove's desk, then gone snap a pic and smirk; like she'd committed a miracle. So when Dove came in an hour before tha doors opened, I started tremblin' and cryin' actin' all scared and what not. Concerned, Dove held me in her arms, rockin' me and askin' what was wrong. Pullin' up my shirt sleeve revealed bruises along wit' a few finger prints trackin' from wrist to inner elbow. "Oh my God!" gasped Dove. "What happened? Who did this?" Water works flowin', I finally stammered out, "I can't, can't tell youuu!" Angry, Dove started pacin' "What do you mean you can't tell me, what happened to our trustin' each other?" She griped. You ever been in school and some kid scratches their nails down a chalkboard? Well dats how listenin' to Dove felt. I 'on't know how much longer I can put up wit' her before I snap, tha switch flips and I stab her to death wit' a spork. I'm just sayin'. I jumped up, "I..I do trust you D..Dove, but I can't I..I'm sorry!" I tearfully exclaimed as I ran from her office. Hey, what can I say, I had a g..good t..teacher, thanks Omaire!   An hour later I heard arguin'. So tiptoein' down tha hall, ears tuned, all I heard was Dove goin' off. "I wanna know what tha hell happened between you mafuckas and Tay'!" Eyes mired in confusion leapt around. "Tay's upset which means I'm fuckin' upset; and ya'll won't like tha fuckin' outcome, believe dat!" she yelled. I'm sure veins were poppin' out all over her forehead. Smirk. "Y'all best bets to tell me now; cause if I hear it from Tay', yo ass is grass. But if you man up right here, right now, I might go a lil easy!" Joe stepped up and cleared his throat so I snuck a lil closer. "I saw Reba and YoYo have words with her. Reba seemed kinda upset and YoYo almost knocked a sandwich from her hands while they spoke. I couldn't hear them, 'cause I was outside smoking." Reba hatefully stared at Joe. "You fuckin' rat! You're makin' shit more than it fuckin' was! If you're gonna tell, then tell how yo ass had her hemmed up in the restroom while coppin' a feel!" Blared Reba, then turned on YoYo. "Don't stand there all smug bitch, 'cause last night while we were at the Russian Lady for happy hour, you told me how you stopped her comin' out the kitchen; how you ain't never like her, don't trust her. How you snatched her up so hard while threatening her you bruised up her arm 'cause she threatened to tell Dove how you up here druggin' hoes so you can rape 'em!" Oh shit! I ain't know 'bout tha rapin' part, ole nasty slut. I know her ass can't get laid, but to take tha pus' while the recipents unconscious is just pitiful okay.

And yeah I let her ass yoke me up, hardest shit I ever had to do was stand there and take that shit; 'cause errbody knows I love to bang a bitch in tha face. Gets my body charged, I'm just sayin'. The tellin' kept goin' back and forth between the two, causin' me to snort kinda loud to keep from laughin' aloud. Hearin' a door open, I ducked across tha hall into tha bathroom, peeked out and felt my eyes widen. Kione. Fuck he doin' here? He stepped into tha office where it sounded like a scuffle was takin' place; and when I heard that heavy ass desk scrape across tha floor, I flew back across tha hall and got my nosy on. And just like I thought, Reba and YoYo were scrappin'. Ump, eyeroll. All that talk and Reba was poundin' YoYo's face okay. I'm like damn homie, break out tha windmill; kick, trip her ass, do some damn thing other then takin' blows to da face. Shit, bob, weave, pay my ass to give you some lessons! I'm just sayin'. "That's enough!" Dove calmly said; and wit' a final punch, Reba backed off breathin' all hard like she'd gone six rounds wit' Tyson. Jog hoe. How 'bout you get friendly wit' a salad every now and 'gin, cause yo ass sound like you're a heart attack waitin' round tha corner. "Joe, Reba you're dismissed." "But Dove.." She whined, a loud slap resonated. "Bitch don't eva in yo life question somethin' I tell yo ass, unless your willin' to take tha repercussions." Gotdamn! I know dat hoe face stingin' like crazy, 'cause it sounded like Dove drew back to west bubble fuck wit' that one, I'm just sayin'. Reba and Joe walked out, eyed my smilin' face and kept it pushin'. I started to go in but somethin' told me not to; and I always go wit' da gut okay. I could hear Dove talkin' to Kione, but couldn't hear jack 'cause ole YoYo was snivelin' and shit. Next thing I know, a shot rings out. Jumpin', I peek in just in time to see YoYo sink to tha floor, blood bloomin' from a hole in her throat. She gasped and gurgled, hands slick wit' blood as she clawed at her throat while her heels thumped against tha floor until all movement ceased. Well damn! I wasn't expectin' that shit right there. Sorry, but that shit was gangsta as hell! Even though I didn't see who shot, tha point is it was done okay; wit' no hesitation, just bam! Take dat bitch! Ooo chile, I can definitely get wit' tha get down okay. Learn 'bout all tha crooked shit Dove and her mysterious partners got goin' on and then take over. First things first, I needed to know where she'd put Sharon and where she was gonna put YoYo.

CHAPTER EIGHT

Life inside the Dark Cavern resumed. I was asked to step up and take YoYo's place until a replacement was found, trained and on board. There were ten hoes includin' Donell and Belinda. Wit' me on board everyone was allowed to roam as long as no one attempted to go outside. I even talked Dove into redecoratin' our rooms. Tha food was upgraded from fries, hotdogs and hamburgers to chicken, steak and fish; I even got a budget for some new hoe gear. I still haven't found any paperwork on who Dove's silent partner is. Did we know each other? Did he or she help put me here? And what'd she tell people when no one saw or heard from me and Glenda? Did she at least put our things in storage? Did she plan on ever lettin' us go? Questions, questions and more questions. Next thing I know, word started spreadin' 'bout some big willie's from a concert out in Wallingford that would be stoppin' through; so these hoes runnin' round like its tha day of their weddin', I'm just sayin'. So I cornered Joe's ass in tha back yard to find out if tha rumors were true. Ole bigums was still salty by tha look on his mug. I'm like really? You wanna be salty, be salty 'bout that face you luggin' round okay bo., I can play connect tha dots wit' all them pus bumps you got all over ya face and that wide ass nose. Bet cho ass can smell a fire six miles away; and hunny chile don't get me started on yo lips. Shit so wide he can whisper in both ears at tha same time. Lips so thick he needs to register for carryin' a weapon, I'm just sayin' a'ight. Anyhoo, Joe was dressed up in khaki pants, penny loafers..hol' up, pause..Penny loafers?! Tha fuck wore them shits anymore? I felt a laugh comin', cause dis ninja done put dimes in tha slots! Ha! Chile I done seen it all now okay. I can go on to glory and rank his ass everyday and never run outta shit to say okay. He'd even shaved dem buckshots he called facial hair. "Got an extra cigarette?" Joe jumped, turned, eyed me like he had some slick shit to say, then pulled a pack of Winston's out breast pocket. Shook one free and passed it, followed by a lighter. "Thanks." Joe nodded and turned back towards tha tree line. "You alright Joe?" Like I gave a rat's ass on whats up wit' his ugly ass. He sighed all heavy like shits really weighin' him down. Here we go. It's obvious he wants to spill it, but he wants me to cojole and sweet talk. He'll be waitin' a hella long time okay, cause Taylor don't baby nobody a'ight. Shit, I'm kid free boo; and if I had one, I still wouldn't do that shit. Fuck

I look like babyin' a full grown silver back, I'm just sayin'. "I'm okay, just hopin' tomorrow goes off without a hitch." "Tomorrow? Whats so special about tomorrow? It's Friday, one of our busiest nights." Ump, I does this boo; no actin' classes required okay. Hell, I'm like a chameleon, I blend in and adapt to any situation. Ask 'bout me bitches cause half ya'll surely need schoolin'. "Yeah, I know; but Dove was over at Hex's club and heard him talkin' 'bout Dirty D performin' in Wallingford. Supposedly they cool, so Hex asked him to stop through. Hex had tha call on speaker, so Dove jumped in and invited his crew to come by and check out the Dark Cavern." Hex. So Dove was hangin' round Hex hunh? "Word, that's whats up, so why you stressin'?" I questioned. Joe dropped finished Winston and crushed it beneath loafered feet. Penny loafers, lmao! "Because Kione's workin' the club with Larry; which just leaves me and Reba, and you of course." He sneered tha latter like I left a bad taste in his mouth. Ooo neva dat boo okay. Dat nasty taste you smackin' on is from yo black ass, swollen gums a'ight. You suck 'em and taste chicken nuggets from last week okay; so don't do me boo a'ight, I'm just sayin'. "Ohh well, why didn't you ask Dove to hire two more just in case? Or she can pair one of tha girls wit' me that night." Joe rolled his joints like tha bitch he is. "Nah, Dove's ass don't trust nobody, so hirin's out; and as for one of the girls workin' with you, that ain't gone work. She needs all pussy on deck." I started to ask did that include Belinda who sucked Joe off every night he's on duty. Or Hannah, who he freaks in tha shower. Acoustics boo, be smart and at least turn on tha damn showers, okay. "Oh well I'm sure things will be okay, you're good at what chu do Joe. Well, I better get back inside." Turnin' I put a lil dip in my back and bounced ass back inside. And sure enough, when Friday rolled around shit became crazy busy. From all tha girls getting' fresh hairdos, mani's and pedi's, Dove personally picked each new outfits, had 'em try 'em on and then decided yay or nay. Then it was onto the kitchen, where everyone cooked or helped prepare food. Wingettes and fish fryin'; and I mean tha good kind, not tha kind Sophie's carryin' round. I ain't neva met a bitch scared of bathwater okay. I remember askin' why she smelled like corn chips, and I never see her comin' from tha shower. Dis fool gone say she almost drowned in tha bathtub when she was eight. First, how tha fuck you almost drown? Bathwater only goes so high befo' it spills over, unless yo ass a midget and standin' at five three; I think not. Second, how you have a panic attack and fall out cause tha showers runnin'? Yo ass at tha sink brushin' yo damn teeth. That's another thang, you panic and fall out wit' shower and bath water runnin', but tha sink doesn't affect you? How so, its still fuckin' water right? Wrong. Let sour pus' tell it a'ight, I'm just sayin'. So no way, I wasn't pickled pig feet touchin', choppin', or stirrin', nothin' I might wanna eat. Anyhoo, Linda made some dip from scratch, hollowed out a brown piece a bread, poured tha dip in, then decorated tha plate wit' celery sticks, carrots, cheese and crackers. Then she wouldn't shut up til I tried it; and honestly, tha dip was really good. Who knew strugglin' edges had it in her, I'm just sayin'. Earlier, Kione had showed up to wax and buff tha floors which he half ass did 'cause he couldn't stop watchin' me. I ignored his ass tha whole time, cause there ain't jack doo doo squat to talk 'bout, ya heard. Darkness fell and Joe and Reba burst through tha door, carryin' bags, cases of beer and top shelf liquor. Restocked tha bar, then Reba sat out colorful candy bowls and filled them wit' weed so strong I smelled it from tha hallway; and a slew of pills, blue ones, peach ones, white ones. Ump! I bet I cop a few of those babies, cause I surely need a buzz to deal wit' Dove's ass okay. Right before tha Cavern's doors opened, dis chick walks in wit' a blonde weave that damn near reached her knees. Her face was done up and dis hoe had slipped in blue eye contacts, okayyy. She wore a cute Tiffany and Co heart necklace; ole copycat bitch, cause I had tha exact same necklace my hubby Mason had copped me. She smelled of Chanel and wore a cute colored boysenberry onepiece wit' furry handcuffs around her waist like a chain belt. My eyes lowered, Zanotti's tha same color as her catsuit. My eyes narrowed, hol' up. Meow bitch, them my mafuckin' heels and if them my heels, I bet a horse pussy dats my mafuckin' got damn necklace! Ooo I knew her ole tasteless behind wanted to be me. Ump damn shame boo, 'cause my gear ain't bringin' yo ass no closer than you are right now to perfection, okay. Only reason her coo coo for affection ass ain't in my clothes is cause her bony body would look like she's wearin' a potato sack a'ight, I'm just sayin'. Tonight, if she bothered to look in any mirror she would realize she looked like a worn down drag queen. "Attention!" Yelled Dove eyes all dilated smile all dreamy lookin'. Heads turned in her direction. "Everythin' looks splendid. Those of you who haven't, go on and change. Tha rest of you get ready, help yoselves to a drink; tonight everyone mingles. We won't be usin' our number system, so if you see somethin' you want, go for it. If he's down, fine, but do not, I repeat, do not under any circumstances start no stupid dumb shit because dude chose a different hoe. Are we clear?" Heads quickly nodded in agreement. "Good. If there's a problem bring it to me, Joe or Reba." Dove spared me a glance before continuin'. "Taylor will be workin' tonight as I have a special request for her, willin' to pay top dollar. Any questions?" Uh.... how 'bout hell to tha yeah! Like when tha hell were you gonna tell my ass 'bout dis special request guess bullshit! What happened to all dat loyalty, let's be honest crap? Ooo tha switch done flipped all tha damn way up okay. Not sayin' I believed her cock and bull story she was slingin' my way, but damn hoe. I see I'mma have to take it to yo ass one more gin m'kay! Dove clapped her claws, drawin' me from thoughts of tap dancin' cross her fuckin' face. "Taylor, can I speak wit' you in private a moment?" Yep, leg go! Once in her office, I slammed tha door and ran up on her so close our noses bumped. "Fuck you on and fuck you mean a special request?" Chest bumpin' Dove, she fell atop tha desk, eyes wide. "What chu got planned bitch, cause Tay don't do surprises, okay!" "Calm down, let me expl.." "I can hear you just fine right where you are; makes it easier fo' me to choke yo neck." I growled, then fingered tha necklace, flipped over tha locket and there it was. "To Taylor the luv of my life, always Mason." "And you got tha balls to wear my shit in my face, hoe you must be bat shit crazy!" Dove burst out in a laugh that would've curled a lesser bitches body fluids. "Okay, you got me." she laughed again. "I'm testin' you. I wanna know once and for all if how you claim you feel 'bout me is true." She spat, eyes wild, crazed. "What tha extra toe havin' ass are you ramblin' 'bout?" And don't think I ain't peep how she jumped from talkin' extra white n proper, pronouncin' all vowels n syllables, but now yo vocab's justa niggerish mess, fake bitch! Ugh! "Come again?" Did I hear her right? Bein' round her I'm startin' to think ole mood swings is rubbin' off on a sista okay, I'm just sayin'. "Can I sit up, please?" Wit' a grunt I took a step back; not too far case I had to do that tap dance I mentioned. "Okay, okay, I..I talked to my doctor; told him how I've fallen in love wit' my bestie and that you feel tha same. He asked how can I be sure? Has she told you he asked. He then suggests I put you to tha test. Of course he didn't suggest this, but I need to know you're for real, that I'm not tha only one whose heart's at stake." Ooo, I could run dat ninja over wit' a garbage truck, reverse a few times til his head looks like red gravy. I'm just sayin'. "So what's tha plan, everytime you don't believe, or trust me or yo doctor?" I threw up quotations. "Ya'll need to test me again, nah boo I ain't wit' it. Fuck it, put me back on tha roster, fuck all dis love bullshit and fuck you too!" Walkin' towards tha door, grin on my face, I ignored all Dove's attempts to have me stay and work things out. Well hot damn! Men of all flavors were walkin' round lookin' gooder den a mug. Just starin' at all dat man meat had a bitch hot, horny and thirsty; and I o'nt mean fo' no beverage okay. Lips smackin', nipples on hard and kitty on patrol as I walked tha room squeezin' a few cakes, caressin' a few balls. Chile I'm in dick nirvana okay. Music started playin' and who strides through tha door wit' an entourage; Dirty D, POPsicle and Dyce. He and Pop were underground rappers but had quite tha followin'. Me personally, I don't wanna hear 'bout a bunch of I gunned down a nigga rat-a-tat-tat-tat, niggas I'll drink yo milk, serve it up big boy style crap. Ninja please, do you not here tha wack shit passin' yo lips, drink yo milk? Homie ya gay a'ight? And if I wanna hear 'bout gunshots, I can sit in my damn window a'ight, I'm just sayin'. Tha girls made a beeline towards 'em like they walked on water. Ugh, give a nucca a few coins and they get tha big head; becomin' all rude n shit like we should be greatful to be in their presense.   Ha! Ask 'bout me boo ,'cause I'll have yo waterhead missin' shows okay. Yo ass won't be able to focus 'cause you to busy blowin' up my phone. Flyin' in to drive pass my crib a'ight, so don't do me boo; 'cause I'll have yo ass mad like a hatter in two point two, m'kay.

CHAPTER NINE

Chile lastnight, ump was a bang and a damn blast okayy! That special guest should've been guests, why? 'Cause it turned out to be none other than Duke n Dee Dee; you know, from the eighties when R&B was tha shizznick. Whoo I used to fien fo' some a Duke's python. I saw them in concert once and baby, ole Duke ain't have on no drawers under his clothes; so that long, beefy snausage was swingin', slidin' and gettin' my juices to flowin'. I swear it stopped a few inches above tha knee. Ump, good Lord give me tha opportunity to ride to tha finish line. To get hit from tha back, hit dese eye sockets and make 'em roll okay; do me right gotdamnit! Of course they both were way over my age cutoff and Dee Dee's ass could sit this one out. Shit, she'd get all in tha damn way, no doubt feelin' some type 'cause I'm devourin' her man and he's lovin' every minute. I'm just sayin'. Babyy ain't no way I'm lettin' Dove interfere wit' me creamin' on dat pole! So I cornered Glenda and Hannah and had them instigate a lil dis agreement between tha girls, then snuck off wit' Duke and Dee Dee, who by tha way looked every bit of seventy. Hmp, damn boo, dye dem roots okay. Shit looks like a silver pot scrubber. Ass'll bite a steak and yo teeth'll stay there, I'm just sayin'; and who tha hell wears flowered mu mu dresses boo, dead old people, that's who okay. Ooo and tha shoes, lorda mercy! Dis chick wore dem orthopedic joints. How tha hell she expected someone to get in tha mood while lookin' at tha mess, that's Dee Dee I couldn't fathom. Now Duke on the other hand was still sexy wit' his low cut silver hair, smooth wrinkle free skin and as he took off them clothes, a body that was still in good shape. Melted knees sunk to tha floor, inhalin' that special scent only a man can have that I'd missed so much. I felt like a fiend on E who'd just copped that first bag of tha day as shaky hands reached out and touched eleven delicious inches, yum! Look out teeth, watch out tongue, open wide cause I'm 'bout to gobble dick and balls, slob, drool, deep throat and gag all in tha name of bein a dick suckin' conesseiur okay. "I'm just gonna watch." she'd said, like I really gave a fuck what she did as long as she stayed out my damn way. Mouth waterin' in rememberence of how tha dick had me wincin' as it stretched and filled my insides to burstin', but in a painfully good way okay. Anyhoo, when Dove finally realized I was missin', I'd got mines; three g's fo' tha pleasure and got tha nuccas phone number too. Like I always say, its what I do boo. Practice makes perfect okay, you can't rush a dick suck wit' a few licks and sucks, a'ight. Befriend tha dick boo, get to know ya new friend a'ight. Ease into things, don't just jump in and start knawin' tha shit; 'cause just like you want tha pus' done right, tha dick commands tha same, I'm just sayin'. Fuck this shit, I ain't Cinderella and Dove ain't my evil stepmother okay. Ever since Duke and Dee Dee, Dove's been throwin' shade in a major way. First she'd suck her teeth or leave tha room, then it was movin' me back in wit' Belinda and Donell. That was fine wit' me, 'cause now she wasn't all up in a bitch face, whinin' 'do you luv me' and 'I know you fucked Duke and Dee Dee, just be honest; I can take it'. Yeah right, yo ass already losin' yo mind hoe. Me tellin' you will have yo ass in a padded cell somewhere droolin', I'm just sayin'. Anyhoo, we sat in her office while she poured her heart out. Poor lil ink tink. Boo get cho life okay; 'cause tha one you gots all over tha fuckin' place okay. One minute you hate me, tha next you wanna be me so you fuck behind me; messy slore. Then you like me, then you kidnap a hoe, then its 'I luv you, I always have', to all these tests; and lets put it all on tha table speeches, chile please. How 'bout you take yo meds on a daily basis? How 'bout some hygiene classes boo? Just cause yo ass dressin' betta don't mean between them slutty thighs are clean okay. Panties so nasty they can walk by themselves a'ight. They so damn hard and crunchy you could throw 'em, bussin' someones head to tha white meat. I'm just sayin'. Yawn, how much longer is dis chick gonna talk got damn. Talk 'bout some shit I wanna hear all damn ready okay. "Dove." I called out; dis nucca kept right on ramblin'. "Dove." I said a lil louder, and again she kept on talkin'. Tha switch jiggled, cause I know she ain't sittin' behind her desk tryin' a do me okay. Queen dirty drawers betta check herself. "Dove!" She halted mid spiel, givin' achin' ears a rest. "What tha hells goin' on wit' you? You've been ramblin', non-stop I must add, since I fuckin' walked in. I've answered yo question boo, a hundred different ways 'cause you asked a hundred different ways." I stood up. "Now either you believe me or not, yo choice; but all dis back and forth crap I'm done hearin' and I'm done speakin' on it, tha balls in yo court." Silence. "You're right." Dove finally responded, eyes bright wit' unshed tears. "I'm sorry, its just I haven't felt this way since sixteen, when I fell for Disco, God bless tha dead." Wait...What? Here I am, thinkin' she and dude parted ways over anotha broad and this Disco person died. Did I miss somethin' 'cause I was tunin' her ass out? "Who's Disco?" A wily look appeared, then faded into one a them 'I know somethin' you don't' looks. Ooo gossip! Spill tha tea hunny cause Taylor loves receivin' all tha news okay. "Disco's Jame's nephew. Remember James?" James, James, shit I done run through the alphabet three times, done had a James seven times; so ole girl needed to be more specific okay, I'm just sayin'. "James is tha one who'd hit tha lotto for $350,000." Ohh, now I remember and chile I was right there helpin' James spend every dollar; and once he was down to less than $25,000 Taylor was out. Chuckle. "Lotto man." Dove nodded. "Right, well Disco was James nephew. Anyway, I caught James in bed wit' Toni. I could've dealt wit' him cheatin' you know, cause all men cheat, it's in their DNA; but to get caught fuckin' a dude was somethin' I couldn't get wit, no matter how much beggin' and explainin' Disco did." Uh hello! Can you blame him? Yo snatch smells like an ass, he probably felt right at home, ha! "So I lured him outta town for a weekend retreat, you know, to see if things were really able to be worked out. Then I threw a few PM's in his glass and bashed his head in wit' a hammer. Whew!" Dove wiped imaginary sweat off her forehead. "You don't know how good it feels to get that off my chest." Lawd dis hoe is bat shit crazy! I thought I had shit wit' me by overdosin' on dick, speakin' my mind and beatin' bitches down when they get it f'd up; but dis right here! What I need is a recorder..a small smile formed. "Me too." Lies boo, all lies. "I'm glad you shared that wit' me Dove, it shows what we have is worth savin', worth buildin' into a strong foundation." Her eyes widened along wit' a smile that showed all thirty-two. "You're so right." she exhaled. "I must trust you and believe in us, because I've never told anyone about Disco." I know yo ass didn't, you might not be workin' wit' a full deck, but chu ain't stupid, far from it in fact. Walkin' behind tha desk I clasped her hand and pulled her from her seat. Fo'give me innards, 'cause I need to keep her ass off balance. Gently cuppin' cheeks, I leaned in and kissed her. Ugh! I think I just threw up in my mouth; although it did make swappin' spit more doable, I'm just sayin'.

CHAPTER TEN

"Joe, can you help me a moment? Please." Baby voice in full effect, I caught Joe and Kione luggin' in a heavy oak, light blue dresser; part of a set for my bedroom that Dove allowed me to move back into. Stunned, Joe froze and almost dropped his end of the dresser. Kione, who's back faced me, grunted then cursed. "Fuck you doin' yo! Bad enough I gotta help carry dat old raggedy hoe's shit!" Ooo no dis havin' sex wit' cho mother, issue havin' bastard didn't! "Uh..sure I'll be right there." stammered Joe, totally ignorin' Kione's bitchin'. Hearin' his words, Kione's head swiveled, then his mouth dropped before swallowin'. To bad yo ass ain't swallow yo fuckin' tongue loser. I sultrily smiled, then slowly nibbled on a finger. "Yo Kione wait here a sec, let me see whats up wit' Tay' right quick." Joe rushed out. "Hol' up, she might need help movin' somethin'. I'll come wit' you." Offered Kione, eyes oglin' tha sheer ruby mid thigh Agent Provocateur baby doll nightie wit' matchin' thong and furry white kitten heels on freshly scraped feet. That's right boo, you got to take care of tha feet okay. Scrape off all tha dead, dry skin boo okay. Don't let it build up 'til you can stroll over burnin' coals and not feel a thang a'ight; and then you got tha nerve to wear sandals, puttin' them joints on display like yo ass done won numerous awards for prettiest feet. And please, please please, take off tha old polish a'ight. Don't pile new on top a old where tha shit doesn't lay right on yo nail okay; and while I'm at it, wear yo shoe size okay. Chile that shit ain't cute okay. Yo ass walkin' round toes draggin' tha damn ground, collectin' rocks, glass and snot some nasty nigga done shot out his nostrils and shit. Be proud of yo twelve's boo a'ight, own ya shit. Now what tha fuck was I sayin'? Oh yeah, I'm smellin' all delicious from Hermes 24' Faubourg and baby, dat shit smells good as hell. Just a dab and it'll attract men in droves and for fifteen hundred a bottle, it better attract a bunch of mafuckas, I'm just sayin'. "Nigga you ain't slick." snarled Joe. "Now back the fuck up before I lay yo ass out!" Kione swung and these two stupid ninjas start scrappin' right in tha damn hallway. I swear, nuccas can be skraight bitches sometimes, cause how ya'll fightin' ova someone who ain't givin' neither one of ya'll a chance to sniff, lick, finger, or stick; I'm just sayin'. Both were landin' blows, but 'cause Joe was taller, his reach was longer; so he'd hit Kione wit' three compared to

Kione's two. Blood dripped from Joe's nose, while Kione's right eye was swollen and closin' fast. Jeez, can ya'll hurry dis shit along befo' Dove pops up, shit. Joe spat out a tooth, roared like a lion, grabbed Kione by tha neck, swung his ass into tha wall and rained down blow after blow until Kione's legs gave out and he slowly sunk to tha floor in a sittin' position. Head still against tha wall, knocked tha fuck out, skraight sleepin', getting' his snore on, catnappin' his ass off; well you get tha picture. Breathin' still escalated, Joe advanced; nose drippin' blood from lips to shirt, his beady eyes jumpin' body part to body part. Can you say flesh crawlin' boys and girls; 'cause that's just what was goin' on as he stared at a sista, ugh! "Sorry 'bout that. Whats sup sexy, why you dressed like that?" He frowned. "You got company comin'?" He suspiciously asked. "Just you lover." I purred. Blah, as if nucca. I'll snack on pus' twenty-four seven if it means layin' down wit' cho beastly ass, I'm just sayin'. He looked shocked, suspicious and turned on all before I could blink once. Stupid, ya'll always thinkin' wit' tha wrong head. That's why women should rule. Ya'll mafuckas fight, shoot and go to war over what we carry between our thighs. "Word?" Ump, it took hella willpower not to back up when Joe got so close I could smell he and Kione's blood, sweat, musty pitts and tha salami grinder he'd had for lunch earlier in tha day; all mixed in wit' tha smell of Winston cigarettes. "Word." I whispered back, then walked fingers from sternum to waistband, glanced up and saw Joe eagerly waitin'; his eyes silently beggin' me to touch, to fondle below his waistline. Tha zippers rasp was loud in my ears, non eager fingers that wanted to knot up slipped inside, found there way inside boxer briefs and my eye twitched in surprise. Well well well, what do ya know, ole Joe here had a nice package between his legs. I played wit' it a sec and when it grew in my hand tha otha eye jumped. Gotdamn! Decisions, decisions! Joe made his pole jump, up, down, side to side, and boasted. "And I know how to work it, I'll have yo ass tappin' out." Ooo a challenge, I loves a challenge! Tha kitty twitched awakenin' from a long ass kat nap. Shit, if I do dis I need a paper bag to slip ova dat mug; 'cause lookin' at him'll dry all tha juices up I'm just sayin'. 'Fuck, let him hit if from tha back!' Shouted tha freak in me. "Hmm, that's what they all say." was all I could think to say while I caressed shaft and balls. That dick heated up, lengthenin' and hardenin'. Suddenly I needed some water. From rubbin' and squeezin' I knew I held nine thick inches wit' a bulbous head. When Joe groaned and moaned out, "Dove won't be here til tonight." I lead him inside by tha ding dong, kicked tha door closed and went for it.

CHAPTER ELEVEN

"Oh shit." I panted. Chile, ole gorilla in tha mist was puttin' in work ya heard! Ump, yes lawd, do my body right gotdamnit! Flip me, "Sss!" twist me, "Uh, fuckk!" Stand me on my head, get all dese snacks okay, tear it up! "Shit, dis pussy amazin'." grunted Joe; diggin' deep, rollin' on top gave a clear view of a face and body pourin' sweat like a heavy rain. Tha dicks good boo, but I ain't tryin' a drown in yo salty sweat okay. Shit drippin' all in my damn eye, got my joint burnin' okay. Shit, if I wanted a shower, I know how to jump my ass in tha tub and take one m'kay; I'm just sayin'. I put hands on a nappy chest, only for 'em to slip and slide 'cause even his chests wet, ugh! Damn nucca, you seriously need a towel. Oh snap, I hope his good strokin', soaked ass ain't 'bout to have a heart attack or a stroke; cause while his ass jerkin' and jumpin' I'll get mines, then roll his ass out in tha hallway fo' Reba or Kione find out, I'm just sayin'. "..So what'd you think?"

Dove and I once again sat in her office. I'm beginnin' to think I need to charge her ass for lendin' an ear while she bitched and moaned. Whoa is me, waah, bitch kill yo'self already and take everyone who's had to listen outta their misery okay. Fuck, I need a damn Tylenol. "Tay', bae did you hear me, what chu think?" Huh? Say what now? "Sorry, I've got a killer headache. What'd you say again?" Keep it short boo, 'cause I'm this close to takin' it to dem flappin' ass lips of yours. "Disco's uncle James' wife Priscilla's brother David's wifey Shirley's sister's datin' some big wig in his country. Anyway, its Shirley sister's engagement party. She's throwin' it on hubby to be's yacht and since its gonna be a lot of dude's friends, she asked if I knew some sexy bitches down for wateva to get that paper. I volunteered tha girls. Do you think it's a good idea? I mean, can we trust the girls not to run, or spill the beans on bein' taken against there will?" Honestly? Who gave a witch's tit, you're the boss hoe, so decide, stick to yo decision and delegate what needs to be done. Me, I'm in there. Last time I was on a boat, it was a day trip spent cruisin' tha dirty ass CT river wit' a bunch a motion sickness riders yakkin' over tha boat and into tha water. Tha shit was gross but when seagulls showed up and started chowin', I damn near hurled my damn self. "Hell yeah it's a good idea. Hell, none of these hoes ever left tha state or seen a boat that wasn't in a picture." "Yacht." said Dove eyebrow arched. "What?" "You said boat, it's a yacht. I'd hate to see mafuckas chucklin' while we're on board; you know how snooty rich assholes can be." Okayy cause my head hurts, I'll let Dove have that one. Mark my words wit' a marker, cause there won't be a second. "Great, its this Saturday; so ask all tha girls what they need. Oh, should Donell and Belinda come too?" Duh, rich mofos from different countries are under cover too dumb ass. "Yeah, they should. So where's dude from?" Clueless eyes looked at me. "Who?" Lord, dis bitch right here. "Shirley's sister's man." Dove shrugged, "Um....Iran, Pakistan, one a dem an's." Wat. Eva. I stood. "A'ight I'ma go get that list started, it'll be ready come mornin'." Dove nodded, lost in her thoughts while underneath her desk she fingered her gushy. Dove trudged through the Buckland Mall out in Manchester on her second trip around the mall searchin' for a store called Bliss that Taylor wanted her clothin' from. Feet and back hurtin', hunger pains knawin' at her belly, she decided to call a halt to her search for a bite of lunch. Selectin' Arbys, Dove ordered an angus burger, medium Pepsi, fry and then found a seat after payin' damn near sixteen bucks for a sandwich, fry and drink. Glancin' around while munchin' on a handful of fries, she spotted two chicks in tha Subway line wit' Bliss bags in hand. Payin' for their food, each gathered a tray and headed towards a free table two tables over. Standin' Dove walked over. "Yes girl, you know I tol' Toby's ass, ah uhn! I ain't cho baby moms, you gone respect me!" The dark skinned, slightly chubby one exclaimed, while the other chewed on her grinder wit' open mouth. "Uh excuse me, hello. This is gonna sound crazy, but can you show me where Bliss is? I've been walkin' round this damn mall for hours it seems with no luck." The two eyed each other, then her. The one who'd chewed like she had no home trainin's left eye continuously cried. "Don't chu see me eatin'?" and "they have directories, can't chu read?" were blurted out at the same time. "Whoa, no need for all that. I'm just askin' 'cause I couldn't locate it, but thanks for nothin'. No wonder we as a people are always downed, its 'cause we can't answer a simple ass question without bein' extra ghetto." Rolling eyes, Dove turned, bypassing tray with uneaten fries and decided to try and see if any stores were on the sides of the foodcourt; when a shove to the back sent her reeling. Just barely catchin' her footing, Dove whirled and caught a fist to the jaw. "Give up tha purse, cash and jewels Barbie." snarled runny eye, while her partner kept an eye out; and since they stood behind a row of big ass plants, no one could see what was goin' on, nor hear with all the noise coming from the foodcourt. Starin' at them both, Dove burst out laughin', "You're jokin' right?" Runny eye punched fist in palm, slowly advancing. "We'll see how hard you laughin' after we beat cho ass and take yo shit!" Throwin' a look her partner's way, Dove had a fleetin' thought if this was how 'Tay' felt that night in the club when she was jumped. "Word? Well run up and handle it, cause I ain't handin' ova shit. Get a job bitch. I would hire y'all, but dat runny eye'll turn off tha horniest nucca." "C'mon Opal." said the lookout. "Snatch that and lets be out." Ole girl's eyes turned back to Dove, catchin' a face full of purse; zipper catchin' her cheek like a serious case of rug burn, followed by a punch to that runny ass eye which moistened knuckles. Opal swung back and the brawl was on. She flung Dove into one of the plants which toppled, hitting ankle and spilling dirt all over Dove's clothing. Ankle throbbin', Dove came out to play wit' a razor pulled from her back pocket and started swingin'; her first swing cuttin' Opal's hand when she threw it up to try and block her face. Dove insanely smiled, fake jabbed and came back lower wit' a swipe across Opal's knee. She screamed as blood gushed from both, finally jarring her friend to jump in and help or pull her to safety. Ole girl did neither, she turned and took off, screamin' bloody murder along the way. Quickly wipin' off prints wit' her shirt, Dove started walkin'; and after passin' tha fourth potted plant, she dropped razor inside, looked up and saw Bliss. "Finally!" Smile wide cause she'd done it, she found tha stupid store all by herself! "Wow!" "Hi welcome to Bliss. I'm Mindy can I help you with anything today?" Startled, Dove stopped gawkin', turned and came face to throat wit' a tall, white chick wit' a purple

Mohawk, nose ring and lip piercin'. "Uh..hi." her eyes lowered, takin' in tattooed 48DD breasts restin' inside a pink fish net bra, her pierced nipples clearly on display. "Uh..I have, I mean my f.." Stammered a flustered Dove. Unclear why she was so nervous, she cleared her throat and tried again. "Shh, first time ehh?" asked Mindy. "Not to worry girl, we have it all. Take a moment to look around and if you have any questions, I'll be behind the counter." "Okay, thanks." "No prob." Mindy walked off swayin' an ass built for a sista. Walkin' around, Dove peeped the harem outfit Tay' had wore months ago hangin' on a rack, along wit' all styles and colors of outfits one could think of. A glass case that stretched the length of the store held cuffs, whips, studded bras, eatable undies and different flavored motion lotions. "Damn, and I thought I was freaky." Dove lowly uttered, eyes glued to a charcoal Grecian style dress wit' slits that stopped just under the pus'. Fingerin' the price tag, she almost gagged six hundred and fifty dollars! Damn did they use gold thread or some shit?! Rememberin' Tay's list, Dove pulled it out, unfolded it and started shoppin'. "Pregnant, your pregnant? When tha hell did you plan on speakin' up? When said baby slid out while performin' a trick?!" I yelled at Glenda. Shit tha only reason her secrets out 'cause I caught her ass eatin' pickles and ice cream. She's sittin' here dunkin' a pickle in vanilla ice cream, lickin' it off, then bitin' tha pickele, nasty! Glenda shrugged, eyes low. "I was gonna tell you when tha time was right Tay'." "Hmm, spit on me and tell me its rainin' girl; and if you do, I'll slap you silly cause that's a figure of speech." Glenda giggled "I know. Are you mad at me?" Sigh. "Nah, so whens my neph due?" Tears blurred her vision at hearin' that. "I don't know, I was snatched before I could make a gyn appointment. Are you gonna tell Dove?" she asked, soundin' all worried. "Hell tha fuck yes. She can have you clean or cook. You don't need to be layin' wit' a trick that likes it rough and he hurts you and tha baby." Glenda hurriedly wiped tears that fell in a rapid pace "Girl, why tha hell are you ballin'?" Glenda walked up and gave me a hug and kiss on tha cheek. "Because you really care about me. Nowadays people say they're your friend but they're really after what ever they can get; be it yo man or yo money." Amen to that shit sista. That's why I hang wit' a select few and even then, them hoes I feed wit' a long handled spoon. "There, there." A'ight hoe, that's enough Maury moments. Back up, got me feelin' all akward n shit. "Thank you Tay'. I'd like you to be my baby's godmother, unless you don't want to." "Sure, no prob." I hope she ain't waitin' on me to start jumpin' and squealin' for joy; 'cause wakin' up in tha middle of tha night to a screamin' baby wit' a shitty, soggy diaper ain't cause fo' celebratin' in my book, I'm just sayin'. "Don't worry 'bout it, let me handle Dove okay?" Glenda nodded, resumed sittin', then picked up her bowl and pickle, ugh! "I'm just askin' why after all this time you feel tha need to want to visit the Dark Cavern?" asked a rattled Dove. She and Hex were at the Olive Garden having lunch. Her shrimp linguine sat chillin' as their discussion had her too nervous to eat; whereas Hex was chowing down on his fettuccine alfredo like he had no worries and hadn't eaten in days. Selfish bastard even ordered a slice of lemon meringue pie. Cold eyes glued her to her seat. "As I recall, we're partners. I check on all my investments, so whats the real problem Dove?" Reaching for her glass of water, Dove almost knocked it over. Catching it just in time, she took a healthy sip then started choking. Hex sat watching her overly dramatic ass try and hack up a kidney to avoid answering his question. "Are you done, or you need me to call 911?" He dryly asked. Freezing mid cough, Dove gave a weak smile. "Sorry; no, no, I'm fine. No need for 911, thanks though." Hex nodded. "Good, because you bein' in the E.R. would put me in charge somewhere you obviously don't want me to be for any amount of time." Dove's fork clattered against her now cold sauce congealing plate. "Uh, that's not true Hex. I'd just like a heads up so you can see tha girls at their best is all." Hex clapped earning a few looks from patrons before returning to there own conversations. "Again, I'm a partner. I don't need to check in with you on anything I decide to do. Are we clear?" Hearing undertones of looming violence, Dove let it go. All she needed was Hex deciding to ask to see paperwork that each woman was supposed to willingly sign, agreeing to work for the Cavern. How much their cut was and so on and so forth. He'd also see his crush Taylor. Mental eyeroll, Hex played like he wasn't interested but she'd seen desire flicker in his eye when Tay' was tha topic, tha way his eyes followed her around tha room. He could fake it all he wanted, but she knew what was what. "Your right, I'm sorry. You can pop up if you like. I was just tryin' to save you from doing so while some, if not all, are on their periods and wit' tha windows closed, its not a pleasant scent." Hex frowned in distaste. 'Gotchu!' Dove exclaimed silently. 'No man wants to hear about or discuss that time of tha month.' "Why don't we stop by after lunch?" Requested Dove, smiling bright. Hex glanced around, not really noticing anything particular. His thoughts turned inward on where the hell was Taylor? It had been five and a half months and he hadn't seen her at work or out and about; nor had she called and when he called her cell it went straight to voicemail. He'd gone over to her place, only to find it empty when he looked inside a curtainless window. Still in denial, Hex had called her home number, only to hear a recorded voice tell him it was no longer in service. Still, he'd stopped some young pregnant chick who told him, 'Who cares wher that trouble makin' bitch went. I hope she stays gone.', before waddling off. Something was definitely up and he planned to find out what. Marcus on the other hand didn't miss Glenda the slightest bit. Since he was workin', he was able to pay Glenda's rent. He'd boxed up all her shit after a month of no shows, no answer of cell phone, then donated everything to the Salvation Army. The apartment was now his and he treated it thusly, creating the ultimate bachelor pad. Monday thru Thursday he brought a chick home, fucked her silly and sent her on her way. Friday nights was poker wit' the fella's night; Saturday and Sunday's he spent doin' whateva suited his mood. Glenda had been getting' a lil to demandin'; 'When are we gonna commit?' 'Do you want a family wit' me?'. On and on the shit went until he was ready to chuck up the deuces and truck it back to Okra; who wasn't a complainer or nagger, she was just happy to have a man in her life. So Glenda not being around was a blessing. Ty felt played. Yeah, his legs no longer worked, but he was still a man; a man who'd broke things off permentently wit' his baby moms which is why she was givin' him hell on seein' his kids. She felt like Ty had led her on, getting' her hopes up when all along he had no plans to be with her for life. He'd done it all for Tay's ass; gettin' her a nice sized rock so she'd know he played no games. Tay held his heart, he didn't care about their age difference. Yeah it bothered him that his shaft wasn't the only one slidin' up inside creamy deliciousness, but Ty figured once she agreed to at least wear the ring, he'd work on the rest. He was being pretty leient when what he really wanted was to shake some sense into her ole stubborn ass. So for Taylor to not answer her phone or to just call him in general was really pissin' him the fuck off. Puffin' an L, something he'd been doin' a lot of lately, Ty decided to give it a few more days before callin' in a favor. Omaire lay abed, idly caressin' a milky white thigh thrown across his leg. His thoughts pleasantly driftin' on nothing in particular when his latest trick said, "How come there aren't any photos of me in here?" Omaire's eyes cut to the right, drinking in Russian Victoria Secret model Katya Glazkov. At twenty-two, Katya was beautiful with shoulder length flaxen hair, perfectly arched brows, pert nose and full lips; her slender 32A 34 24 frame was taut, full of ropy muscles from daily workouts every morning at five a.m. Katya didn't have much ass which he liked, hell even her breasts were less than a handful which Omaire didn't too much care for either. What he did like was Katya's complancy to keep Omaire satisfied until now. Katya knew all about Taylor, that she was her replacement only. Katya had no intention on going anywhere, now or later. "What?" Katya eyed a eight by twelve sitting atop Omaire's dresser of Omaire happily smiling, arms wrapped around Taylor THE BITCH. "I ask why are there no pics of me here Omaire." It took Omaire a second to filter through her accent to get the meat and potatoes of what Katya had said. "No reason. I just never thought about it."

replied Omaire. No longer thigh rubbing he sat up, swung legs outta bed, stood and crossed the floor; naked cheeks flexing, dick bobbing. Katya hungrily licked her lips as light blue eyes watched his every move. Pouting, Katya slid from the bed and met up with Omaire right before he closed the bathroom door in her face. "Ya nenavizhu tibya." lashed Katya; light blues flashing. Omaire understood and spoke a few different languages, Patois, Italian and a lil Chinese; so truthfully Omaire didn't understand any of what Katya said, but the anger on her face and in her eyes gave her away. Omaire snatched her ass up. "What? Say it in English bitch!" He snarled, more angry at Tay' disappearing than Katya's jealousy. "I say I hate you Omaire! You treat me bad, unless you want sex." Squeezing her arms, Omaire grilled her from head to toe, then smirked at hard nipples. "Yeah, y..you h..hate me so m..much yo n..nipples are hard." Omaire leaned in and nibbled Katya's ear. "And I..I bet that p..pussy s..soaked ain't it?" Cuppin' her breast, Omaire tweaked her nipple, snaked down between Katya's legs and felt an ocean coat hand and wrist. Slowly pulling free Omaire sucked his finger clean his eyes never losing contact. Katya moaned and shivered, then yelped in surprise when Omaire whirled her around, kicked her legs apart and ordered, "T..touch ya t..toes." Doing as told, Katya bent and felt her eyes roll when Omaire thrust inside to the hilt. "Oh, oh yess Omaire. Ya tibya lybulyu." she chanted, matching every thrust teeth biting bottom lip. Harder, deeper, Omaire gripped slim hips making sure her shit talking ass couldn't get away as he blew her back out. "English!" Grunted Omaire, slapping cheeks so hard he left five a fingered inprint behind. "I...I said I luv you Omaire. I luv you so much." whined Katya, eyes tearful. Omaire ignored all that shit she was talking 'cause good dick had hoes falling every day. One last thrust and on the outstroke Omaire pulled free; grunting when Katya clenched pussy muscles trying to keep him inside. Whirling, her back facing him, Omaire put palm atop her head and pushed, the universal signal for suck my dick and do it well. Katya eagerly complied. Mouth wide, she greedily cleaned up all her juices, sucking and licking him like her favorite candy back home in Russia. "Sshitt!" Roared Omaire. Katya wasn't able to deep throat like Tay', but she did a damn good job at what she could do with a dick; for now at least the topic of Taylor was no more.

CHAPTER TWELVE

Damn! Ole Tiphanie had become tha Dark Cavern's biggest money maker. Who knew she had it in her. Maybe that dope knew, cause her ass done a complete three sixty out chere, I'm just sayin'. She no longer carried around a bucket of flab, she'd slimmed down to maybe a size sixteen, eighteen; had learned how to apply make-up and even let Glenda cut her hair in a cute asymmetrical bob, then dyed it honey blonde wit' light blue streaks. Ump, you go girl; 'cause you damn sure needed some help boo okay; 'cause from head to toe was tow' up from tha floor up, a'ight. I don't know how Brian's dick slangin' behind even got between them cottage cheesy thighs. Probably had to oil her ass up so he wouldn't chafe and stick like glue. She was also a pure fiend. Dove had to smack her ass twice 'cause she's in her room suckin' and fuckin' fo' a bag, so tha custie was comin' off wit' extra; especially since her dumb ass was askin' once tha deed was done. I'm just sayin', if you gone fiend, be a smart fiend okay. You always handle business before pleasure m'kay. Dumb weak hoes, I swear. Anyhoo, tonights tha yacht party and I can't wait. Dove finally made an appearance three hours before our departure; mouth tuned to tha whoa is me channel. I gave tha hoe tha turn and strut, 'cause greatness had to get ready okay. Two and a half hours later and I was lookin' like tha delicious diva I am okay; fab-u-lous hunny, ask 'bout me. Hair up in a messy bun wit' wispy tendrils on nape, face beat to tha make-up gawds, smellin' all good in Joel Rosenthal's 'Jar Bolt of Lightening'. Crazy name I know, but that shit smelled so divine I knew I was a walkin', talkin', switchin' orgasm causin' bitch by smell alone. Wearin' a begonia colored, stoppin' at my cootchie, off one shoulder, sides cut out so I couldn't wear a thong, Bliss dress and Julien MacDonald spike heeled stilettos; Taylor Janae James stepped on tha scene critically eyin' them hoes to see if any were halfway on my level. Nope, not a one, I'm just sayin'. Dove stepped up wearin' a purple Emilio Pucci fitted dress. It was cute and kinda reminded me of tha fad when chicks wore latex dresses, which I let pass me right on by cause why in tha hell do I wanna walk around lookin' like a pair of surgical gloves or a damn condom lubed up and reat to go, I'm just sayin'. Outside two limos sat idlin'; ugly ass Reba behind the wheel of number one, ole Kione behind number two. Eww, I hadn't seen him since Joe fucked him up in tha hallway. Just tha thought had a bitch cheesin'. Ump, damn that had been some good ass dick ole Joe served up. Smackin' lips, I slid into Kione's limo just because; gapped thighs and caught his ass droolin' in tha rearview. "You a'ight boo? 'Cause you lookin' kinda thirsty." Smirk. "Fuck you Tay'. Fuck you jump yo hoe ass in here for anyway? Ride with Reba and Dove since you like to ride anythin' wit' a pulse. One day yo triflin' ass gone ride tha wrong one and end up catchin' AIDS bitch!" He spat damn near foamin' at tha mouth. First tha shit was funny; then I realized Kione's ass wished death on me. Oh no boo, you've done tossed grease on tha fire! Linda slid in beside me yappin' 'bout my dress, but tha switch done flipped okay, so Ms. Linda will get her turn in a minute. "Who ugly? Hol' up, pause and hit rewind boo; 'cause yo ass done jumped off tha crazy train if you think I'm gonna let tha shit you spat float in tha air and marinate. You done bumped yo huge ass head on tha steerin' wheel, okay. First off, don't be J cause I don't wanna fuck yo ass, stupid. In case you forgot I'm your momma, much as I hate sayin' them words. What we did was a mistake, a big fuckin' mistake; so get over yo self all damn ready. Second, Tay' can ride in whichever limo she pleases and yo backed up sperm carryin' ass ain't gone do shit but shut up and drive, cause I cuts kids boo, okay. Third, dis good ole snappa can ride tha north pole if I wanna and you can't do shit but cry, sulk, jerk off and act like tha lil bitch you are m'kay. I can't help it if da snatch shrivels up and trys to crawl up inside me at tha thought of you whippin' out cho man meat, okay. Fourth, I checks out tha goods on a regular basis boo okay. Whenever I decide to ride bareback is no one's business but mines; and tha dick I'm enjoyin'. Of course yo ass knows nothin' 'bout pleasure or enjoyment when it's in tha same sentence as sex huh? Hmm, yo ass ain't neva seen, smelled, sniffed or tasted hunh? You's a damn sexually frustrated asshole ain't chu boo?" Linda, Hannah and Tiphanie had slid into a seat, heard me goin' off and were laughin' their asses off. Linda was in tears, Hannah held her side and Tiphanie's ass jumped out shoutin' 'I gotta pee!' Hilarious! Kione's ass ain't say shit. He sat there jaw twistin' when we finally pulled off. A huge ass yacht called Amor was already teamin' wit' people when we rolled up. Now I've been on a yacht before, but babyy this shit made Omaire's look like a damn tug boat, I'm just sayin'. Ump, my lips twisted from tha sight of ghetto trash strollin' round like they owned tha yacht when they should've owned a tasteful outfit okay. 'Cause dirty, worn dollar store flip flops, ragged, holey shorts and sundresses that showed sunken in ass and cellulite stomachs wit' huge floppy arms ain't tha way to go, a'ight. Shit, I'd never pass 'em Dr. Crawford's number and have him call to curse me out cause her body was unable to be fixed, I'm just sayin'. Dove walked over to this monstrosity wearin' a blonde wig that did nothin' fo' her face and dark complexion; along wit' that sundress was a complete no no okay. They hugged and started in our direction. "Girls, this is Tammy. Her sister Shirley invited us, wit' Tammy's okay of course. Tammy these are tha girls. Ladies behave, enjoy and if anythin' kicks off I'll be down in tha pool room." Eyin' me fo' a piece had tha switch jigglin'; 'cause why you bring my black ass if its gone be all a that message witcho eyes bullshit. I'm just sayin'. Soo Tammy's hubby to be was one ugly micky flicky okay. Chile he so ugly, he walked in a haunted house and came out wit' a job; so ugly he makes blind kids cry. I'm just sayin'. Dude was dressed nice, I'll give him that, in charcoal colored Apo jeans and Azzaro shirt; I just can't get ova dat face. Hmp, looks like tha lord just threw some pieces togetha and called it a face okay. Tammy walked around latched onto dude's arm, stoppin' long enough to introduce him as Nurul Bayu and to brag he was from Indonesia and very wealthy before continuin' her stroll. Really? Rich and no taste, damn shame okay. Then again, his face and her fucked up frame; I guess they were made for each other, I'm just sayin'. Amor was five floors of luxury. Basketball court, helicopter pad, movie theater, fifteen rooms decorated in gold trimmin', jacuzzi's, a room wit' five pool tables and more, just skraight snazzy a'ight. Ole Nurul hopefully has a rich brother on board, 'cause I could surely get used to this shit here. Glenda and I ended up in a dinin' room wit' a long ass ash grey colored table full of mafuckas laughin' and talkin'. So wit' Glenda glued to my side, we headed towards another table, set up buffet style. Servers stood at tha ready, smiles bright, willin' to slice succulent meats or to answer any questions on what dishes were displayed. I only recognized a few items, like whole steamed lobsters and crab legs; oh and I spotted grilled chicken too. "Eww what's that gross shit?" Glenda asked, face all frowned up. I started to elbow her ass but I ain't want her kid comin' out all lopsided and get tha shit blamed on me, I'm just sayin'. She's my road dawg, but tha hoe is so uncouth. Some piss colored, buck toothed chick snootily answered, "These?". She hovered a nail so damn long on her index finger it curled and twisted all crazy, endin' up facin' her palm. Gross ass, bet not be no boogers under that shit and they fallin over tha food like seasonin'. Shit so long it takes three bottles of nail polish to paint one damn nail, I'm just sayin'. Tunin' back in, I heard, "That's hervido; which is a beef soup with potatoes and other vegetables. This is chivo al coco, which is goat meat cooked in coconut milk and served with mofongo; that's fried, mashed, green bananas and this,..." she took three steps to tha left, "is Jamaican dishes."

sniffed like one of us stank and said, "Which I'm sure you recognize." I did, but who asked twisty nail to prance her fuckin' ass over here and insert herself in our convo; and is tha bitch tryin' a sneak diss Jamaicans and their dishes? Tha switch jiggled. Glenda knew how I am, so a quick shake of her head and a clutch of my arm, followed by a harshly whispered, "Be cool Tay'. We don't wanna be thrown off and we just got here." Damn, she's right. So playin' nice I politely smiled. "These are Moroccan, which is my favorite. That's charmoula, stuffed sardines, Marrakesh, a veggie curry." she smacked lips so thin they were damn near non-existant. "Very delicious, that's Italian." which she strolled right by. "These dishes are Russian; coulibiac, which is a fish loaf." Glenda farted, I pinched her arm. "Sorry." she lowly whispered. "It just sounded nasty as hell, fish loaf." Glenda shuddered. ".....And pelmeni, which are dumplings; and last but not least, my second fav, Indonesian dishes. That's bakso, a savory noodle meatball soup; and padang, a goopy curry with floating fish heads and rubbery cow's feet. And there you have it. I'm Rebecca by the way, enjoy your meal ladies." We watched ole Rebecca make herself a bowl of padang, selected some stuffed sardines and sauntered off. We burst out laughin'. "Gurl, I ain't know how much longer I could keep from laughin' in her saddity ass, stick like face." "Right. Well c'mon, lets get our shit before Rebecca pops up wit' a lesson on where and how to sit." Commented Glenda. "Would you like to play a game?" Chills ran down my back, raisin' all kinda goosebumps at hearin' those words. Ooo, you askin' tha right one boo. What we playin'? 'Cause Tay' loves tha sex games okay. Blindfolds, fruit eatin' off yo body, tickle yo ass wit' a feather, I'm just sayin'. "Excuse me." Turnin' put me face to chest wit' a sexy, bald head, gleamin' hazelnut colored gawd. He grinned, revealin' pearly skraight whites behind thick, full lips. "Pool, would you like to play a game of pool with me?" Damn, and he smelled good too. Aww sukey! Eyin' his frame from head to toe, I had to cross my legs to keep snatch from clawin' free, pouncin' and goin' fo' hers, I'm just sayin'. "And what will we be playin' for?" Hint, hint, sexy. "I'm Wulan, and we can play for whatever thou desires." Ump, can somebody turn down tha heat 'cause tha thongs sweatin' boo, a'ight. My nipples all hard and ready fo' some tongue action, followed by a slow lick downstairs okay; cause tha way Wulan's lickin' his lips, I can tell he's a master cunninglus I'm just sayin'. 'Cause not everyone can find one or pick 'em out a crowd, but Taylor's a pro boo, okay. I can sniff out a footlong, blink and know if yo pockets on E, among otha things a'ight. "Really?" Givin' a quick look around I then got right up on his body, raised my hand and rested it against firm chest; ran it down hard, ridged six pack, over belt buckle and hovered over zipper. Eyes locked, his light browns hypnotizin' like a snake wit' a rabbit before lowerin' and finally runnin' over firm, hard, ding dong that twitched beneath my grip. "If I win?" I gave a soft squeeze, a small smirk appeared. "You American women are very outspoken, I'm beginning to like it. So if I win what do I get?" "I'm Taylor boo, what would you like?" Wulan reached out and cupped a tit and slowly drug his finger over distended nipple. Ooo yess boo, flick it, bite it, stick tha whole damn thang in yo mouth okay, I'm just sayin'. "Yo wish has been granted." Turnin' back to tha pool table, I watched Wulan select two pool sticks, chalk and strode back wit' a mean ass confident walk that turned me on anew. Yess Wulan, I wanna undress you boo and lick you all ova okay; and I wanna nibble that nutmeat til' yo neurons no longer fire, a'ight. Fuck wit' me, I'll suck out every last drop okay boo; til' yo eyes roll and you done fo'got how to speak English. "Thanks," I purred, starin' him down. Wulan passed stick and chalk; I sneakily felt tha tip and estimated it was a medium soft. Oh, chu ain't know, ump. I'm a bitch of all trades a'ight; and if I ain't I'll adapt and still come out on top. Ask 'bout me boo, cause you done bit off more than you can handle. Wulan racked tha eighteen pool balls. "Eight ball?" Wulan asked. "Sure boo, let's do this." Big grin splittin' sexy lips, Wulan offered, "Ladies first." "And you know dis boo. Try not to cry when you're horribly beaten by a woman." Yeah I'm cocky andd? "We shall see Taylor. We shall see." Smirkin', I walked up to tha table, tooted out an ass that still looked good nine months later, lined up my shot and bam! I hit tha shot, ball one rolled smoothly into its home, smirk. "Solid." Wulan nodded, leanin' over I gave a wiggle, lined it up and POW! Ump, I can feel his tongue smackin' on clit already. Hold on kitty, momma's got this. I'm just statin' facts. Back in my Mason days, well before tha armored truck robbery, Mason would teach me somethin' new. We'd practice til' I got it, then move onto somethin' else. I fell in love wit' playin' pool 'cause Mason would lean up against me, bendin' my body; positionin' my hands while hard dick would poke me in tha ass. Shit, half tha time I couldn't concentrate nor remember what Mason had said and shown me, too focused on that hot, hard, muscle promptin' me to drop my panties and re-assume position. Three shots in I purposely missed tha next two. After all, we were drawin' a crowd, some even placed bets; so I figured don't slaughter Wulan, he might be so destroyed when its time for a different game, his wiener might be outta commission. I'm just sayin'. A few of his Indonesian brethren shouted out what I assumed were words of encouragement, since whatever they said wasn't in English. "Eighty bucks on my girl Tay'!" Yelled Glenda, instigatin' by wavin' four twenties over her head. Ole cheap ass. Girl please, whip out some big bucks boo a'ight. Let's take dick, jewelry, money, I want it all okay; 'cause Taylor's greedy okay. Ain't no shame in this forty-nine year olds game ya heard. I had two balls left, Wulan six. Aww sukey, I'm down to tha ball sac boo, tha gristle. Ooo and I do so love to nibble on tha gristle. What..oh chu don't know? Hmp, let cho inner freak out boo; maybe then yo man'll stop sweatin' me, I'm just sayin'.

CHAPTER THIRTEEN

"Your chocolate skin is so soft." said Wulan between kissin' and nibblin' my collar bone. "So sweet." he added latchin' onto pebble hard nipple, Yeah yeah. Shit gets sweeta tha lower you go, so hurry tha hell up and let me satisify yo sweet tooth boo. Wulan swirled tongue around navel before slidin' lower. Plump mound, meet lips; lips, enjoy tha sweetest, juiciest, creamiest fruit you'll ever taste in yo life. Beware boo okay, 'cause you 'bout to tread in dangerous waters; and I can't and won't be held liable when you lose yo mind okay, I'm just sayin'. Umm, okay now. Gone and get it, lap it all up boo. My legs splayed wide, one leg went up, restin' on Wulan's shoulder; tha other I took by tha ankle and pulled it skraight back 'til toes touched my ear. That's right, I'm a flexible forty-nine boo; don't hate. Smackin' and suckin' noises rang out loud and clear for a nosy, paro bitch like Dove who'd listen at every door to see if she heard me behind it. Hips undulatin', my eyes closed in pleasure. "Yess boo. Ohh that feels so good." I moaned out and it did; 'cause next thing I know I'm coatin' Wulan's mouth and tongue. When he rose, his mouth was all glazed; his tongue swept out and got every drop. My eyes stretched so wide, I waited on 'em to pop out and hit tha bed. Hot grease on a bald scalp! Wulan's tongue was long as fuck okay. Shit so long I don't know how he closed his mouth without chokin'. "Lay down boo, let momma return tha favor." I whispered. 'Cause again, I don't want ole owl ears to hear me before I get to taste and ride those eight inches standin' at attention, oozin' pre cum. Yummy! We switched roles and I was on it like a tick burrowin' under skin okay. Mmm, smellin' fresh, bump free. A slow lick from base to tip on one side, a tongue swirl suck around tha head, I froze. Ugh! Tha fuck? Why Wulan's cum taste like clumpy ass, spoiled cottage cheese? Fuck he been eatin'? I let go so quick tha dick sprang back and smacked pubic hairs and belly. Wulan's eyes popped open to see me steppin' into thong, lips twisted. "What's wrong? Why'd you stop?" Was he serious, why'd I stop!? How 'bout cause that's tha worse cum I ever tasted and I've tasted quite a few okay. A lot and not once have I tasted somethin' so disgustin' in my damn life! "Uh, I stopped 'cause yo insides need a serious cleanin' boo. Yo shit all clumpy. Fucks that about? And why it taste all sour and curdled okay? I pride myself on bein' tha best okay. I'm a dick conneseur a'ight, but that dick right there's way beneath my dick suckin' skills okay. So whatchu need to do boo is see a damn doctor, a urologist, somethin'." I spat. Now dressed I gave one last look and strode to tha door, gave a booty clap and walked out. "Whats the matter princess?" Questioned Katya's father Lyev as they ate breakfast. Shrugging, Katya pushed a boiled egg around her plate. "Is mother here?" Lyev replied, "No. Katya I wish you would work a little harder at forgiving your mother. Now tell your father what is wrong?" "Well, I really thought Omaire liked me. I mean, I'm a Victoria's Secret model and they only use the best. So why can't he see that I'd be good for him and him for me?" "Aww honey, I'm sure this Omaire guy, who I've yet to meet by the way, cares about you. How could he not? You're beautiful, caring, intelligent; just give it time, I'm sure he'll see the big picture." Smiling, Katya reached across the table and patted her father's hand. Omaire opened the door welcoming his guest with a handshake. "Glad y..you could m..make it H..Hector." Deep dimples on display, Hector returned the handshake and upped it with added pat on the back. "No problem, how's Kitty?" Omaire chuckled. Hector, who'd gone to school with Omaire, had always had it bad for his mother Kitty. "D..doing w..well. Traveling, tha u..usual." stuttered Omaire as they walked out on the patio where Omaire's maid would serve them lunch. Omaire knew if anyone could locate Taylor it would be Hector. After all, he was a top notch private investigator whose services were requested world wide. Jackie, a cocoa brown, svelte woman walked out, tray in hand. "This is your maid?" Joked Hector with a wiggle of brows. Omaire chuckled as Jackie served a lunch of homemade beef soup, turkey sandwiches and tall frosted glasses of iced lemonade, lemon wedges decorating rims of the glass. "So whats up Omaire? You and I haven't seen nor talked to each other in what... six years, give or take?" Asked Hector before biting into sandwich. Omaire did the same, trying to get his thoughts in order before answering. "Y..your're right, a..and I a..a..apologize f..for that; but I..I n..need your he..help." Sipping sweet, cold lemonade Hector processed Omaire's words. "Go on." Omaire hesitated, then did just that; and when it was all said and done, Hector eagerly agreed to help his friend Omaire locate his fiancée Taylor. Ty was pissed as he rode his wheelchair back and forth, simulating someone pacing. Sucka ass Smokie stood before him, left eye black and blue; bottom lip congealed. "Smokie my man." voiced Ty through voicebox. Smokie nervously nodded, not trusting himself to burst out screaming and apologizing from the Challenger exploding to Isis' bombing. All he knew is one moment he was asleep and the next he'd been snatched from bed, pummeled, dragged from his grandma's house where he slept in the basement and thrown in the trunk. Smokie thought this was the end and began praying. When the car finally stopped and the trunk opened; and he realized where he was, he wished it was anywhere but there. Smokie knew Ty wasn't big time like before his shooting, but he still dabbled here and there; plus, the nigga had friends, if one could call brutal murderers friends. Smokie tightened sphincter muscles, "Uh..hey Ty. W..whats up man?" Smokie nervously stammered, wanting to wipe rivers of sweat from his brow; but scared it might be construed as reaching which in turn might set off Kayden and Rick, two of Ty's dirt doers. "That's a good question. I'm gonna ask a question Smokie and it would behoove you to answer truthfully; we both know how I feel about liars." Smokie felt like he'd swallowed his Adams apple and was ready to release it out the other end any minute. "Okay." rushed out over dry tongue and swollen lips. "Smart choice. Word is you have a problem with a very good friend of mines." "Sorry, sorry Ty. You know me man, I would never.." "Cut the crap!" Dried up every word Smokie was gonna say. "I need you to find this friend for me Smokie; and when you do, you call me. You do this right and you'll be set for life." Smokie immediately relaxed. "Sure, sure. Who you want me to find Ty?" Ty smiled. "My fiancée, Taylor James."

CHAPTER FOURTEEN

Well that sneaky bitch! Angry at myself for not findin' what I sought sooner, when tha shit was right under my nose. Dove's sneaky behind had taped a manila envelope on tha desk's underside. Not knowin' when she'd appear, I carefully unsealed tha envelope and pulled out around six sheets of paper. Tha first was a sheet wit' all tha hoes names includin' mines; tha dates and where we were taken from neatly handwritten on it. Sharon's name had a red line through it wit' a date, which I'd never fo'get. Tha next was an itemized bill from Holmes Creatorium. Jaw clenchin', ooo that tramp had fried Sharon! Fuckin' heartless skank! Bingo! Tha remainin' four sheets were ownership of tha buildin' and her silent partners signature sat right beside hers. Hex. Quickly slidin' tha papers back, I stuck it back where I'd gotten it, stood and speed walked out her office. "I don't know Tay'. I can get in serious trouble." Joe harshly whispered. Frustrated, I stared at

Joe's punk ass. Ump, mighty funny how his ass wasn't scared or worryin' 'bout getting' caught when I slipped his ass some pus' okay; but now I need a lil fava and dis nigga buckin' like I asked him to help me escape. Punk ass! "Oh word?" Fake tears started fallin'. "I thought you felt for me, what I felt for you Joe. I know now it was all just to get in my panties, its okay. I'll ask Reba, or Kione for help." I kept my voice anger free, which was hard as fuck. I'm not a passive chick okay and I've played nice long a damn 'nough. Wit' a last sniff, I turned, head down lookin' all dejected n shit; and what do you know, ole Joe has a change of heart. "Alright, tomorrow. Same time." a hard glare, "Don't make me regret it Tay'." Ignornin' his weak ass warnin', I hugged him, gave a quick peck of lips and raced out tha closet/storage room I was in when I first entered tha Cavern's doors and back to my room. Glenda was now seven months and eatin' twenty-four seven. Of course Dove refused to turn Glenda loose, citin' Glenda would send tha law. So instead, she pulled her from hoein' and gave her kitchen duties instead. I couldn't wait for darkness to fall. Joe's ass better show and have what I asked for; 'cause I'll flip tha switch and spin it all around when I tell Dove everythin'. That's right, I'll snitch on Joe's ass so damn fast I'll get myself dizzy okay. A bitch needs her life back okay. Shit, I can't even enjoy tha ass I paid for cause its locked away n shit, so its do or die time a'ight and cause mofos got loose lips I ain't told nobody nothin'. Five minutes before showtime, dressed in boy shorts, sports bra and flip flops, my hair up in a ponytail; I grabbed a soda out tha fridge and almost jumped out my skin when I closed tha door. Dove stood there, eyes full of suspicion. "Hey, whatchu doin'?" "Uh..gettin' a soda. Why whats up?" Dove glanced at her watch. "It's late, can't sleep." Tha fucks up wit' tha twenty questions. Shruggin', I popped tha top and took a healthy dose, burped nice and loud. Dove wrinkled her nose. "Excuse you. Anyway, lets talk in yo room." she said. Aww shit, either her ass wanted sex or she knew I was up to no good. Fuck! Dis bitch fuckin' up my plans; I swear its always somethin' or somebody. Poutin', angry, I followed; makin' faces at her back n shit. Once inside, Dove flopped on tha bed, laid back and got comfortable; then patted tha space beside her. Rollin' eyes, I finished my soda then slowly joined her. "Do I treat you good Tay'?" Hell naw hoe! I'm here against my fuckin' will dumb ass. "I mean, you've got yo own room; which I let you decorate how you chose. I took you off hoe detail, I even gave you time to decide about us." "And yo point is?" Came out slick as hell. "Tha point is, I know you fucked dude on tha yacht; and I know you've been leadin' me on, but no more lies, no more games Tay'." Dove coldly stated. "And? So? Whatchu want, me to beg you to believe me? Shit, yo minds already made up, so do whatchu gotta do." Dove smirked, "I'm so glad you feel that way boo." she mocked, snapped her fingers twice and in walked Reba and ole smirkin' ass Kione. Great. Just fuckin' great. Big shit eatin' grin on his face, Kione strode in like king cock. Bastard. "Take Taylor to tha room." she ordered. Wit a wink and flap of tongue, I eagerly followed behind bodyguards, mentally cursin' out Joe's ass.

CHAPTER FIFTEEN

Not sure how long I sat in that room, hungry, nose wrinkled in disgust from tha shit and urine mixture emanating from tha bucket. I'm hungry, I'm tired, I smell and I'm ready to slice Dove's damn throat as soon as I'm free and I'm gonna step to Hex's ass too; ole fake ass nigga and all his 'We cool Tay's and come work for me; Mason was my boy, I'm a make sure you skraight.' Say goodnight hoe, cause everytime I see yo face you got problems. Tha door unlocked. "Psst, Tay'." Joe! I jumped up and trotted seven steps over. "Here. I couldn't get whatchu wanted, so use mines, hurry up." Whispered Joe, then closed tha door. A cheap flip phone lay in hand. Ump, its been so long since I saw a damn phone, I kept rubbin' it before rememberin' I'm supposed to be makin' a call, flipped it up and stared at lit screen and number pad. It's true, you never miss it til its gone okay. Joe tapped on tha door. "Shit." I mumbled, tryin' a remember anyones number; eyes squeezed shut so tight I saw all types a colors before a number popped in. Dialin', it started ringin', and ringin'. "C'mon, c'mon. Pick up damn it!" Know hopin' I dialed it right, my fingers crossed. It went to voicemail. "Yo, I..I can't c.come to tha p..p.phone right n.now. Leave a m..message a..and I'll hitchu back." soon as I heard stutterin' I sighed in relief. "Omaire, its Tay'. I'm bein' held boo, I need you....its a place called tha Dark Cavern.." The door opened, "Times up." he harshly whispered. Noddin', I ended tha call and handed Joe back his phone, neglectin' to tell him I didn't block his number before dialin'. Katya stared at the phone indecision dancing in her eyes, Omaire was in the shower singing off key as she reached out and plucked it from the nightstand. The message light was blinking, pressing voicemail, Katya thanked Omaire for forgetting to lock his phone. "You have one new message; Omaire, its 'Tay' I'm bein' held boo, I need you..its a place called tha Dark Cavern.." To save message press one, to delete message press seven." Katya quickly pressed seven just as Omaire cut off the water. Quickly placing it back exactly how he'd left it, the door opened and out he walked surrounded by a cloud of steam. Omaire eyed her. "Why y..yo a..ass so j..jumpy?" "Not jumpy, horny." purred Katya, throwing off blanket and parting legs. Omaire smirked, strode over to his phone and picked it up. Katya's heart pounded in fear and excitement. Fear because of what he'd do to her if he found out what she'd just done and excitement because she wanted to see his reaction after that choke sex session in the bathroom she had discovered she liked; a lil pain thrown in the mix. He licked lips. "T..temptin', but I h..have to pass r..right n..n..now." stammered Omaire as he pulled boxers and wifebeater out his armoire. Feet kicking in anger, Katya quickly flew from bed and pounced on Omaire's back and started swinging. "S..stop! Katya w..w..whats w..wrong wit' you!" Bellowed Omaire, then flipped Katya over his shoulder. She landed on the bed, bounced and hit the floor knocking the wind from her lungs. Wheezing, Katya stared up at Omaire nonchalantly getting dressed; no doubt preparing to go see about his precious Taylor. With a last look, Omaire strode from the room. "But why daddy?" whined Katya with a stomp of foot. Nikolay Glazkov sighed and rolled eyes behind the morning paper. Katya was spoiled beyond repair, always wanting more and more outrageous things and usually he'd grant her wish if it wasn't too outlandish; and this request was just that. Katya wanted him to use his connections to put feelers out on locating someone named Taylor James. Yes, he could grant her wish but what concerned him was what Katya wanted to do with her after locating her. Katya wanted Taylor to be sold overseas on the sex trade market. "Katya ," Nikolay lowered the newspaper and glared at his daughter, "do you know this woman? And what has she done to you for you to want to do this? And if I were to help you Katya and this Taylor woman found a way to contact someone back in the U.S. and everything leads back to me, I'd be in tons of trouble and probably in danger as well. Is that what you want Katya?" Katya sucked her teeth, then stood her chair scraping against expensive tile. Nikolay watched his only child stride angrily from the dining room; his hopes low on Katya who was an eternal hot head following his advice. Moved from closet back to tha room where I'd been tied up upon tha bed, Reba's ole smug ass appeared, steamin' bowl in hand. I ain't trust this cow not to have spit in that shit, but a bitch starvin' and I need all my strength, energy and wits; so right now I needed to trust I wouldn't croak or have tha shits behind this broad. "Well hello. How's our fallen from grace hoe doin' today?" Snort. Like dis bitch really wished someone would pay her ass half tha attention I got. Ole jealous, hatin'beotch. "Aww whats tha matter boo? You mad 'cause you can't pull a john no matter how hard you try? If you ask me nicely, I can upgrade yo look boo." I started to do her ass, but at tha moment I need her, which stuck in my craw somethin' serious. Reba smiled; showin' off a bottom row of f'd up teeth and gums. Eww, no wonder she never smiled, ump; teeth so yellow, I can't believe its not butter. Teeth so fucked up she can eat through a chain link fence. Shit so crooked she gotta suck a dick sideways, I'm just sayin'. I could see all over her mug she's interested, so I smiled again and said, "It sure smells good." then opened wide. Reba approached, picked up the spoon restin' inside and scooped up what looked to be beef stew and rice. Stomach rumblin' in anticipation, Reba cleared her throat. "Did you mean it? That you'd help me upgrade my look?" Chewin' carrots, potatoes and meat never tasted so damn good. I eyed Reba from head to toe. Ump, first thing to go boo is them run over Reeboks okay; 'cause them shits is leanin' way left a'ight. Looks like you walkin' on tha sides of yo fuckin' feet okay. And what size boat she wearin'? Shit look like at least a thirteen. Ump you got extra toes too in them shits? I'm just sayin' and them faded, big ass pants look like she wearin' Andre the Giants pants; and them country ass cuffs her asss rockin's no better okay. Shit makes no damn sense. I'm like do you pass a mirror at any time durin' tha day? Chile, and please don't get me started on that rat's nest atop her head, I'm just sayin'. "Yeah I meant it Reba. I know we started off on tha wrong foot, but I ain't got no beef witchu; so if you want my help I'm willin'." Damn, bowls almost empty. Suddenly Reba frowned. "And whats in it for you, if I were to agree?" How 'bout a dentist visit boo, 'cause yo breath's hummin' a damn tune okay, jeezus! "Nothin'..maybe someone to talk to, it gets lonely bein' locked away." I meekly replied. Reba slowly nodded. "I can definitely relate." I betcho ass can hunny, I betchu can. Hex hung up the phone after sending out a few 'keep yo eyes and ears open' demands. He'd heard from his old friend Smokie, well his jump off Alice's son Smoke, and what he'd relayed had Hex biting his lip in anger. True, he and Taylor weren't an item; shit, in her book they weren't even friends. Taylor was there for the money and the money only, so why did he care so much about how she was, where she was and if she'd ever let the past go so he could take care of her in all ways? Pouring a healthy amount of whiskey, Hex tossed it back with a grimace, then called this nigga Ty who Smokie claimed was also looking for 'Tay'. Maybe they could pool resources because somebody out there knew something.

CHAPTER SIXTEEN

"Answer tha phone. I asked you over to help out, not bitch and moan. You can take off if that's what you came here for." ordered Ty as he sat at kitchen table munching on crab legs. Briana Jefferson, his sometime errand runner and dick sucker stood, foot tapping. "Ever since you got a lil feelin' back and can get a hard on, you've become a real dick you know that." Spat Briana. Ty sucked his teeth and gritted, "If you don't answer that, I'll hurt cho ass Briana." She snatched it up and barked, "What!?" Ty wiped his hands, then grabbed a steak knife. "I'm sorry. I mean hello, Ty Hamilton's residence." then eyed Ty. "It's some guy that stutters, says his name is Omaire and that you two have a common interest you should discuss." His eyebrow rose. "Ask him who, cause I don't discuss shit wit' niggas I don't know." Briana quickly did as told; she hoped and prayed that it was bad news on that old bitch Taylor; that way she could console her man to be. True to my word, I helped Reba's ass out; and lord knows it was a humongous undertakin' okay. We started wit' them feet and chile, I almost hurled when she pulled off her sock. Them joints had a thick pad of dry, hard skin on tha heels she oculd crack bricks on okay. So I showed her how to take better care of 'em, asked her favorite color and then had her buy some real nail polish and not that cheap ninety-nine cent shit out tha hair store. From there I moved onto outfits; after I explained it's alright to snack, but not all day everyday on bullshit. After that, I asked to use her cell phone. It surprised my ass when Reba happily agreed. Well damn, if I knew it was that easy I would've been befriended her sad, lonely ass; I'm just sayin'. "H..hello?" "Oh my God, Omaire. It's Taylor!" I yelled all hype while excitement of bein' rescued danced in my veins. "T..Taylor!" Omaire yelled back, ringin' my ears. I'll cuss him out 'bout that once a bitch free. "Yes boo, in tha flesh comin' to you live from tha Cavern, did you get my message? Whats takin' so long for you to get here?" Rattled off, not givin' Omaire a chance to reply; and when he finally did, I ain't know what tha hell to say. Dis ninja gone stutter and say, 'What message?' Ooo he's askin' for tha switch to flip okay. Don't play me crazy boo a'ight. I might be old, but a bitch ain't senile. He lucky I ain't got time to argue cause tha switch's jigglin' okay. I'm just sayin'. "Look, I can't stay on tha phone. I'm at a hoe house called Tha Dark

Cavern, come get me nucca." "W..what tha Dark C..Cavern? A'ight c..calm down. I'm o..on it." Click, cause that's all I needs to hear okay. If his ass ever wants to sample these snacks and mouth game again, get on tha job ninja. Shocked, Omaire stood stiff, brain working overtime. 'What were the odds that he was on his way to meet up wit' the mysterious Ty regardin' Tay', only for Tay' to call?' he mused. 'Was this a trick to get him somewhere and rob him? Or worse, hold him for ransom? It wouldn't be out of the spectrum of reality. Afterall, his father was the rapper Kidd who still had millions at his disposal; millions he'd willingly spend to resuce his only child. Stopping at hallway closet, Omaire grabbed a lock box off the shelf, reached into trench coat pocket and pulled out its key. Minutes later, Glock 17 fully loaded on his waist, Omaire set off to find out if it was a set up. Briana and Ty sat inside Mickey's Drive Thru at separate tables; she chowing down on fried clams and onion rings, their famous handmade milkshake, strawberry her favorite, waiting to be guzzled. Ty sipped on a slushy citing he wasn't hungry. Briana watched him check his Audemars for the third time when they hadn't even been there six minutes yet. Hell, her fingers and toes were crossed anyway in hopes that stuttering homes didn't show. That way she could do a lil 'let me make you feel better' moves. All that sunk to the floor when in walked a fine ass specimen who favored the rapper Kidd. Panties soaked, Briana watched him looking around, then did a lil finger wave when their eyes met and added a pinky point at Ty who caught her movement and peeped dude and his gun he tried to hide beneath his shirt, stride in his direction. Omaire strode over, waitin' for dude to stand and give tha hood handshake until he realized dude was seated in a wheelchair; so he reached across the table instead of striding around, that way dude didn't think he was on some bullshit. Ty shook his hand wit' a strong secure grip, which surprised Omaire since he thought all wheelchair riders were on the flimsy useless side like their legs. Omaire slid into a seat and eyed dis Ty character, and when he picked up some kinda gadget and held it to his neck, his jaw dropped in surprise. "Sup, you Omaire?" 'That shit sounded crazy as fuck' thought Omaire as he nodded, "Y..yeah, you T.. Ty?" He questioned in turn as Ty thought, 'Dis stutterin' nigga here. No way he satisifying Tay'; probably fucks like he stutters.' The two talked, feelin' each other out before relaxin' enough to bring tha topic of their comin' together to the table; and before it was all said and done Ty and Omaire came together to go get Taylor..... and then to make her ass decide who she wanted to be wit'.

CHAPTER SEVENTEEN

The Dark Cavern was open and business was boomin'. Tits, ass and balls were jigglin' from men, women; men and women pretendin' to be women, as more custies pulled up, eager and ready to unload Friday's paychecks weighin' down their pockets. Dressed to impress as always, I sashayed around ignorin' Dove's eyes borin' holes into my damn back; hopin' Omaire arrived soon. I pulled Glenda to tha side when she came waddlin' from tha kitchen wit' Buffalo wings and bacon stuffed mushrooms, lettin' her know hopefully our rescue was immenent. Mafuckas were eatin' like they hadn't in days okay, just skraight greedy. They asses could've been eatin' cat, munchin' on doo doo balls n shit; which would serve 'em right for eatin' from people you know nothin' about, I'm just sayin'. Offers for a piece of alla dis greatness was turned down 'cause I wanted to see every minute of my resuce, pounce on Dove, then happily skip my ass back to doin' what I do best, get my fuck on okay. I waited, mingled, waited, flirted and waited some damn more. I'm sayin', how hard is it to come get a bitch!? Did tha hoe fly me to tha moon or some shit? Fuck it, drastic times call for desperate measures, its time to give ole Reba a dose of Taylor and have dis bitch walk me and Glenda outta dis mofo when her shift starts; cause a bitch can't depend on a mafucka for nothin' but a bunch a damn lies okay. 'Bae I'll be there in twenty. I'm starvin' whip daddy up somethin', only for his ass not to show or call. Then has tha nerve to show up a day lata like shits good, or how 'bout 'we goin' out I gotta show my bae off, put on somethin' sexy'; and when he shows fourty five minutes before it closes, he's pissy drunk and not capable of shit but sleepin' it off, I'm just sayin'. "I'm tellin' y'all, ain't no fuckin' Dark Cavern in Hartford!" yelled Briana. Tired, hungry and horny, she'd been up all night callin' around askin' everyone she could think of if they'd heard of or been to this place. She'd flipped through white and yellow pages til her eyes burned from lack of sleep. All she wanted was a lil appreciation. A thanks would be nice but nooo, Ty was bein' his usual dick headed self and she was sick and tired of it. "Bitch watch yo mouf fo' I buss you in it." bassed Ty. Only it didn't sound any different from his usual tone. "M..maybe she's not in H..Hartford." commented Omaire which halted all arguing between the two. "Well did Tay' say where she was?" Asked a frustrated Ty. Omaire racked his brain as he tried to remember every word Tay' had spoken upon his answering the phone. "N..no s..she was b..b..bein' rushed t..to h..hurry up; l..like s..she'd snuck and c..called. M..maybe T..T..Tay assumed she's s..still in H..Hartford." Silence fell. Ty wheeled over to his fridge and grabbed two Heinkens. 'Gee, thanks for askin' but no thanks, it's too early for a beer.' Briana sarcastically thought, nails agitatedly tappin' atop the kitchen table; a loud yawn slid free. Briana stood and trudged toward the living room for a nap on the ocuch. Ty watched her go, debatin' on puttin' her ass out. Omaire cracked open his beer, jarring Ty from thoughts of Briana keepin' info from him and wringin' her neck to get the whole story past her lyin' lips. I caught up wit' Reba in tha backyard doin' squats n shit on her hour break. I'll give her credit, she stuck to tha script, at least 'round me and I could see tha results. No way was her ass anywhere near my lane, but it was a definite improvement. Dove had been stayin' out my face, thank God; so I know now's tha time to do this shit. Glenda told me she overheard Dove talkin' to Hex on tha phone. He was done listenin' to her excuses on why everytime he wanted to come through, her ass was nowhere around; and without havin' his own set of keys he couldn't get in, unless he visited durin' business hours. Even then, if Dove was MIA, he'd have to pay like everyone else as no one knew about her 'silent partner'. Sounds good, but I can't keep sittin' on my ass waitin' on Hex to catch up wit' Dove and make an appearance so I'd be set free. Plus, who's to say that nigga wasn't down from tha start and helped put my ass here. No, Reba was my chance and I'm takin' it. Fuck it, if I gotta nibble on a nipple and lick sum pus', so be it. Freedom. The air was definitely fresher on the outside. He stood still for a moment or two, letting it all soak in. No more screams and cries at night from newbies being welcomed by a dick shoved up their ass. No more clanging cells and jingling keys as guards walked the halls ignoring those same screams of innocence forever lost. A cream Land Rover rolled up, jarring him from those thoughts. Having left everything behind as he wanted nothing to remind him of his stay, he popped the collar on a crisp John Varvatos shirt, gave a quick glance to black Rampage jeans to make sure they laid right over his bresciani socks and Valentino shoes; then stepped off the curb, opened the passenger door and got in. Big Sean played at a decent level about 'Ass'. His sunk into cushion soft leather seats that swiveled, massaged and were heated. His eyes took in all the dash's gadgets as when he'd gone away none of it was out; then cut to the left where cold, but happy to see him black eyes took him in. He'd never been a scrawny nigga, but he'd gotten his weight up and hardened it into muscle and strength. Where once lay a hairless face, now sat a low cut, beard sharply edged up. No more dreads hung, behind the wall they couldn't be kept up the way he desired; so now there sat a low cut with some serious waves. In his ear and around neck and wrist sat jewelry that was sent with his clothing and shoes; even a bottle of Jean Paul Gaultier had been thoughtfully included. The two rapped knuckles. "Lookin' good my nucca, welcum back." drawled Nugget, who'd been released seven years prior. "My nucca." he replied. "It's good to be back. Nice ride by the way." Nugget smiled. "Glad you like it, its yours. I cleaned her up yesterday since she's been chillin' in storage. Slid in a new battery, you know, the works." Nugget jumped on the highway headed back to Hartford. "I gotchu a place to stay too, wanna swing by there first?" "Nah, run me to the Courts. I gotta scoop wifey outta that shit, then we'll go." Replied Mason, heart beating fast from the thought of seeing Taylor after all these years. Mason and Nugget sat observing Nelton Courts going's on's. "Do you see shorty?" asked Nugget; blowing billows of smoke from Black & Mild, eyes glued to a chick sauntering past with ass cheeks hanging out a pair of shorts so short it could've been panties. "Nah." Mason rolled down the windows, "Yo! You in the yellow top! C'mere!" called Mason. Nugget chuckled when said yellow shirt saw who was calling and raced over damn near falling when she tripped over her feet. "Damn, shorty thirsty as hell." chided Nugget watching her near. "Shut up nigga, for she hear yo crazy ass." said Mason, doing his best not to join in. Rosalie stopped at passenger door and leaned down, putting 40D's on display. "Heller, and how may I assist yo fione ass?" Battin' lashes, Rosalie spared the driver a glance, determined he wasn't cute enough and resumed gawking at Mason. "Whats yo name?" Mason questioned, then ran a finger between clefted breasts. Rosalie shivered and had to swallow to keep from drooling. "R..Rosalie and you?" Mason smiled, he started to suck his finger and reel her in, but when he pulled it free it came out saturated with breast sweat. "Nugget." Nugget's head whipped in their direction. Beaming, Rosalie gave a girly giggle; in actuality it sounded more like a moose's mating call. "You got a number Rosalie?" 'Damn.' she thought. 'I can't wait to hook up and brag to everybody. Too bad Tay's ass ain't been around.' "Sure." Mason glanced at Nugget who grudgingly pulled out his own cell while muttering, "We're stoppin' at Verizon." before handing it over. Rosalie quickly rolled off her digits and started prattling on about nothing, until Nugget mentioned they needed to go. So wit' a promise to call, they pulled off.

CHAPTER EIGHTEEN

"I don't know Taylor. If we're caught we'll catch hell from Dove. I don't need or want to get on that bitch's bad side. Please don't be mad." said Reba. Is this moo cow serious! Don't be mad, trick please, cause I'm way past mad boo okay. "So all that we cool, if I need anythin', what was all dat?" Lips smackin', neck and eyes rollin' I stared at Reba like she had two damn heads m'kay. Hell, she needed two cause tha one she's got is just takin' up space, fuckin' skag. I'm just sayin' cause here I am, ready to seal tha deal wit' a lil licky tha splity and dis bird gone punk out. Jeezus, am I tha only one wit' heart up in dis mafucka!? "A'ight, just remember yo decision boo; 'cause I will get outta here and every mafucka who did me wrong is added to my payback list." Turnin', I walked off, ignorin' all dem 'Please Tay lets talk.' and 'Don't be like that please'. Hoe, please talk to tha back okay. Dressed to impress, Rosalie got ready for her date dreamy smile on her face as Toni, Kelly and

Brick grilled her. Ignornin' all that, Rosalie almost came on herself from a knock at the door. Toni and Kelly, who was due any day, ran to the door eager to see who had mom dukes so excited. When Toni swung it open, both girls eyes popped wide at the sight of Mason. Each had thoughts of twerkin' on his pole, hookin' his fine ass and leavin' Brick to console their mother. Before Mason could introduce himself, Rosalie stepped up, elbowin' both girls who blocked her exit. "Close y'all dick lickers, tah tah." and strode arm in arm down the sidewalk, steps falterin' at the sight of Mason's friend whose name she couldn't remember behind tha wheel. "Oh..I thought we were goin' out together?" Mason smiled. "We are. My license's suspended, so my boys gonna drive us." Smiling back, Rosalie eagerly slid into tha backseat. Her heart skipped when he slid in beside her, dampening her panties when warm palm rested atop her knee. "So." Rosalie croaked, cleared her throat and tried again. "So, uhm, where we headed?" While mentally crossing fingers that it was over to his place to get her back blown out; and by the look of him, ole Nugget looked like he put in work. "A nice lil jazz spot I know. They serve some delicious soul food." Nodding, Rosalie nervously shifted in her seat; unsure what to say and do as her dates, which was a rare damn occurance, usually involved her cookin', restin' on her knees, gettin' dicked from tha back and a promise to call that never came. Twenty minutes later they pulled up at a small restaurant downtown that she'd ridden by numerous times and never noticed called Mary's. "Nu..Mason, come back in two hours." Nugget whose name for the time being was Mason when around Rosalie nodded and pulled off. he'd spend the time wit' his Puerto Rican mommy Jessica. Mary's was nice. The employees were jolly and very helpful, which had Rosalie stumped. She was used to gum chewin' and attitude when her order was taken; although she did feel some type when she peeped how overly pleasant their waitress who fawned all over her soon to be man. Having had enough, Rosalie spat, "Can you take our orders before closin'?" The waitress turned a fiery red and hurriedly did as requested; already on her second write up and she'd be standing in the unemployment line. Now alone and feeling tons better, Rosalie sipped her sweetened iced tea looked up and froze. "What's the matter?" Mason sighed. "I don't like the shit you pulled ma. I got no claim on you and vice versa. That young ladies eighteen, way too young for me. Control that jealous bullshit or I walk, ending this date before it even gets started, understood?" Mason coldly snapped. Chastened, Rosalie meekly nodded in agreement. "Good, so how long you lived in the Courts?" Glad he was no longer feelin' some type of way, Rosalie eagerly answered, "Fifteen years. I'm originally from Boston." Mason pleasantly smiled. "Oh, so you probably know a lot of characters down there." Rosalie snorted, "Do I ever! We got 'em all in the courts; from fiends wit' no shame, thieves who'll steal yo undies off tha line, knock on yo door and try an sell 'em back; and then there's Taylor who some call Tay'." Mason perked up. "Oh yeah. Whats wrong with her?" Again Rosalie snorted. Their food arrived; cabbage with hamhocks and a side of porgies, while Mason had greens with smoked turkey legs, mac n cheese and jerk chicken. "You were saying?" "Oh, Tay's a hot mess. Anytime there's drama in tha Courts, nine outta ten she's in it, or was tha cause of it. For instance, she'll go off on you and then swing. Tay's a fighter be it man or woman; she'll also fuck whomever she pleases and tell you to yo face how it was." At first, Mason felt a huge surge of anger that the next mofo had laid between his wife's silky thighs, then reality slid in and he relaxed. "She sounds like a wild one." Rosalie laughed, "You have no idea." A band took to the stage introducing themselves as Palin and began playing, Rosalie who wasn't a fan of jazz or blues, found herself head bobbing along to the rhythem. "This is nice, thank you for the invite." "You're welcome. So are you friends with Taylor?" "Hell no, I don't trust Tay' as far as I can throw her. We chat, but all that other stuff, no way. Besides, no ones seen Tay' in months. Dove came and emptied her and Glenda's apartments." His brow rose. "And no one thought to question it?" Rosalie shrugged. "Not really. Dove, Glenda and Tay' are friends." Mason chewed on a homemade dinner roll. "Wow, I'm glad I don't have friends like y'all. If it came down to it and you were in a jam, I'm sure you'd want someone to care about where you disappeared to." "True. But enough 'bout tha Courts, tell me 'bout you." she purred. Mason bit into his piece of chicken. "Well, I recently was discharged from prison. I'm searching for someone." "Really, well who? I'd be glad to help you in anyway I can." Rosalie gushed. Mason smiled. "Glad to hear it." Rosalie reached across the table and clasped Mason' hand. "Who Nugget? Who's tha lucky person that you want back in your life?" "Taylor. My wife." "How'd yo date go playboy?" Joked Nugget. "Man, that birds beyond desperate for a mans affection; but after a lil persuain I found out Taylor and a friend disappeared after rumors started that this Dove chick opened a hoe house, supposedly called The Dark Cavern." "Good name." said Nugget. "Yeah." Mason fired up a cherry flavored Black & Mild, having been unable to smoke in prison after a no smoking policy was implemented. He took joy in freely puffing. "So what's the plan?" "We need to find dis chick Dove and find out where this Dark Cavern's located; rescue my wife and lay down anyone who sees a problem with that." Nugget nodded in agreement. "I'm wit' it. Let me make a few calls, see what I can dig up. Give me til the morning." "Done." Kione sat in the dark, lit cigarette the only light in the room when he inhaled. Guilt was eating him alive for what he'd done to his mother. He realized too late that it wasn't her fault he'd grown into the man he'd become. He'd just wanted to meet her, to find out why she'd left him instead of raising him as a mother should. Having sex with her had been awesome, but when reality set in he knew it was wrong. No normal human being would pretend to be a stranger just to get in their mothers panties; and then he helped send her to a hoe house. What kind of son was he? She hadn't done anything to deserve that. Hell, he hadn't even given her the proper chance to be his mother before he'd ruined everything. Maybe he could make it right and start anew. Crushing out his cigarette, Kione contemplated on how to do so without making the situation worse than it already was. Maybe this was his chance to show Taylor he was sorry and wanted to start over. The next time he went to work at The Dark Cavern he'd sneak his mom out and whisk her away to safety. She'd have to forgive him and give their relationship another chance then. Feeling better, Kione stood and went to bed.

CHAPTER NINETEEN

This was it. Glenda's due date was quicktly approachin'. Tha plan was to catch Reba when she went in tha bathroom, knock her ass out and swipe tha keys; wait until tha hall was clear and make a break for it. Yeah, that's all I got, so I gotta at least try. Dove was also supposedly outta town. It's all good, cause once I'm free I'll definitely come back to visit. "Give it up Tay', please. Let's just wait 'til someone comes. I'm pregnant and can't help you take down Reba." pleaded Glenda. "Girl I got this. All I need you to do is sneak tha rollin' pin out tha kitchen, pass it to me and I'll do tha rest." Indecision covered her face. "I don't know Tay'..." "Glenda don't make tha switch flip, 'cause I go off on pregnant chicks too okay boo. So relax yoself, eat some gross food and take a nap." Glenda laughed, but I'm serious as hell. "Okay Reba comes in on Thursday; hopefully tha two-day grace period will have you re-thinkin' some things." Wednesday morning Nugget had the info on Dove and The

Dark Cavern. Along with a pleasant surprise that bought a shit eating grin to his face. Hex was in Hartford and not only that, he was a partner in Dove's business, how interesting. The nigga had a niteclub and a strip club, so Mason called Rosalie and had her call both to see if his ass was there. No luck at the strip club as no one answered, but at Hexagon he'd be in at eleven. And at precisely ten fifty-nine, Nugget and Mason made an appearance at Hexagon. Both ignored the bartender who'd just entered the room carrying a box of glasses as he shouted from across the room, "Sorry, clubs closed til tonight. You can come back then." Nugget pulled out a chair and had a seat, while Mason met dude on his way to the bar. "I'm looking for Hex, the owner." "Hex isn't here; and even if he were, you still can't walk in here demanding shit." griped Adam, setting box atop bar counter only to turn and connect with a fist that sat him on his ass. "I advise yo ass to stay down. This ain't got shit to do with you, but if you get up, it will be." Mason calmly stated. Wide eyed and pissed that he let dude get the drop on him, Adam slowly pulled his poker, a Mora Fire knife from his back pocket and came up swinging just as Hex came through the door. Nugget sat calmly watching the show. He peeped Hex enter; saw the confusion switch to surprise at realizing who stood in his club and what was taking place. Mason took a step back and to the right, as Adam lunged with a "mother fucker!", only for a loud yelp to escape when that same wrist twisted and bent back til knuckles touched wrist. Adam's yelp escalated to screams of horror and pain as his hand uselessly flapped back and forth. Hex shouted, "Wait!" and made a beeline towards the ruckus, only to be snatched up by Nugget. Mason picked up and pocketed Adam's knife, turned and eyed a non struggling Hex. "Sup Hex, long time no see. I see you're doing well." Hex tried to stay cool. He knew Mason and Nugget were dangerous and probably even more so after he'd sang like a canary on amphetamines, earning himself a get outta jail with serving less time card. "H..hey Mason, N..Nugget." stammered Hex. "We need to talk Hex, lead the way to your office." demanded Mason, then snatched a moaning, crying, snotty faced Adam and walked him along. Ty and Omaire drove around to all the after hour places, hit up a few gambling spots and put the word out on Dove's hoe house and if the info panned out, the reward would be great. The shit was frustrating. Six one one had no phone listing, it wasn't listed in phone book or on the internet. Ty finally suggested Omaire ask some of his rich minions, as they might have heard of or visted. Omaire could've kicked himself for not thinking of it first, then hastily did just that. An hour later, Omaire got word that it was either in Beacon Falls or Easton Connecticut. The gentleman who'd been, had gotten pretty inebriated and didn't remember which. Thursday morning dawned a dismal grey.

Dark clouds rolled in obscuring what lil sun fought to stay revelant; it looked like six p.m. instead of seven in the a.m. That shit felt like it was it was a sign of oncoming doom. Stretching, pulling boy shorts outta crack, I threw on my bathrobe and strolled down the hall; passing Linda and Sophie along tha way. Tha bathroom stood empty except for Tiphanie, who leaned against tha sink tightenin' a belt around her arm; needle full of breakfast sittin' inside tha soap dish. My lips curled. "Damn gurl, you gotta do that hot shit in here?" I griped. I mean come on, everybody knows Dove done turned you out on dope; but now yo ass eagerly does whateva to obtain it.Shit, you givin' hoes a bad rap wit' all that noddin', scratchin', droolin' shit okay. Damn boo, can you remember yo past life and at least make an attempt to go cold turkey? Don't get me wrong, I know it ain't easy. I remember my cousin Tyre's boy Derick's baby momma Ebony's momma Hazel was on that shit and chile, she was a hot damn mess a'ight. "Yeah, Larry just got here. Nigga knows I need my fuckin' fix." bitched Tiphanie. Grabbin' needle in one hand, she placed it between her lips, flexed belted arm, gave it a few slaps, then slowly inserted tha tip into a vein. Ooo watchin' that gave my ass tha heebie jeebies fo' real! "Is Dove here?' I asked. 'Cause she and Larry the midget were fuckin' and from what I'm hearin', dude loves to pillow talk, before durin' and afta; so Tip' would definitely know. I knew it was only a matter of time before multiple personality would show up buggin' and I needed to be long gone, I'm just sayin'. Tiphanie's eyes rolled and her head started wobblin' around on her damn neck like one a them bobble toys people stick on there dashboard. "Tiphanie." Snappin' fingers by her ear earned a listless smile. "Helloo Tay' to Tiphanie. Can you hear me girl?" Dis chick starts moanin' n shit, opens her robe and starts caressin' breasts, then down to her snatch where she jams in four fingers and starts hunchin'! Aww hell naw! Fuck outta here wit' dis horny bullshit. I don't wanna watch yo ass get off, nor smell tha scent emanatin' from between her thighs. "Nasty bitch." I muttered and went into a stall to pee, hopin' that grey skies and sloppy pussy weren't a sign of things to come. I'm just sayin'. 9 A.M. Nobody in Beacon Falls were willing to talk or were really clueless on the questions asked as Omaire sat inside a rinky dink trailer looking restaurant titled Tom's Diner. Frustrated, Omaire stared at a few customers, the majority being what looked like truck drivers and old people that looked like even Viagra couldn't get a rise out of. The bell over the door jingled and in walked a younger, spiky haired white boy. "You're late." growled dude stationed at the grill. A cheeky grin appeared, along with a bop in his step. "Sorry Tom, me and the fellas had a long night out celebrating Willie's twenty first birthday at this whore house." he whistled in appreciation, then made womens curves with his hands. "Rich you and Willie wouldn't know what to do with a woman, let alone at a house of pleasure." joked one of the truckers, sitting three seats down from Omaire at the counter. Ears perked, Omaire laid down fork, wanting to hear every word ole Rich had to say. Tom cut eyes in Omaire's direction and met hard stare before he looked back at the grill. 'I knew these cracker, red neck bastards knew something', thought Omaire. Rich went on and on as he stood behind the counter gathering dirty glasses, plates etc. before refreshing empty coffee and tea mugs. "Ha ha Pete, sorry to disappoint but I handled myself very well thank you." boasted Rich. The bell chimed and in walked a cop. All talk immediately ceased at his arrival, which pissed Omaire off. Here he was, minutes away from finding his fiancée and in walks a fuckin' pig. Fuck! Omaire peeped his tag as he sauntered by, leather boots clipping the ground as if itching to tear into the dark meat sitting at the counter; making his way to a booth in back, which gave him full view of the entire eatery. Usually the sight of the law would have him going quickly in the opposite direction, but the urge to rescue Taylor overrode all that. Omaire realized as he sat there, that he loved Taylor; that he was ready to settle down with her, to possibly even get her to agree to having a baby. Rich strode around the counter, took Officer Wright's order, gave it to Tom and headed to the restrooms also located in back. Omaire stood and slowly followed. Nugget fiddled with a fancy shamcy letter opener, not realizing until he saw the inscription on the handle that ole Hex knew Dove. Mason sat behind Hex's massive desk, Hex sat in a chair in front of his desk. "Where's Taylor?" Hex shrugged. "Your guess is good as mines. She hasn't been to work, nor called me. Is something wrong? Did something happen to her?!" Hex said and jumped from his seat, only for Nugget to shove him back in it. "Don't move nigga; fo' you find yo dick gift wrapped 'round yo neck." Ordered Nugget, letter opener tightly held in hand. "I'm asking the questions." Mason calmly stated. "What'd you mean by Taylor hasn't been to work? You got my wife stripping and hoeing for you nigga?" Feeling the shadow of death tapping his shoulder he gulped. "L..look Mason, man I know we've got bad blood between us." Nugget smacked the back of his head. "I mean between the three of us, but you've gotta believe me. I would never hurt Tay' or have her out her living wrong; so I hired her to work here at my club. She promoted my club on radio, by word of mouth and flyers and that's it, I swear." Sweat started rolling down his back from the heat of an intense stare from Mason and Nugget. "You swear? Nigga fuck outta here, you swore once before remember." taunted Nugget. "W..wait! Yes, I fucked up and I apologize for that; that was the old me. I've matured, I'm trying to live my life right. I swear I don't know where Taylor is." Hex rushed out, tripping over his words in his haste to get his point across. "Whats The Dark Cavern?" Questioned Mason, grilling Hex for any signs of deception. "The Dark Cavern?" Confused from the jump in conversation, it took Hex a second to reply, then rapidly spit out an answer when Nugget gave his neck a painful squeeze. "I'm part owner!" Gasped Hex, then rubbed the back of his tingling neck muscles. "With who?" Mason already knew who, but he wanted to hear if Hex would own the truth. "A friend of Taylor's name of Dove, Dove Mitchell." "And where can I find dis bitch?" barked Nugget. "I'm telling you bra, if something happened to my sis I'ma kill yo ass, give you CPR and do it again." he promised. Hex released a silent puff of gas that smelled like rotten eggs. "You nasty ass mafucka!" yelled Nugget waving letter opener hand before his face. "Sorry, sorry, I'm nervous; I..I couldn't help it!" Hex tearfully shouted, then shot a glance at Adam who sat on the floor; eyes closed, arm tucked against his side. "Adam! Ask Adam; he and Tay' had words a few times and my..my boy Larry Love too." Said Hex throwing both under the bus. Adam's eyes popped open and widened in horror at seeing Nugget hovering over him, sneakered foot raised and ready to stomp broken wrist. "You got somethin' you wanna share Adam? 'Cause that wrists lookin' fucked up. Then again, I can give you a matchin' set." Promised Nugget. Gulping, Adam squealed and burst out crying in fear. "Fuck you man! Fuck you

Hex!" Both Mason and Nugget eyed each other as memories of Hex doing the same shit to them re-surfaced. "Fuck all that blubberin' nigga fo' I give yo ass a reason to fuckin' cry." Snapped Nugget, while Mason calmly sat observing. "Okay!" Yelled Adam. "Me and Larry felt some type after the way Taylor acted all fuckin' superior, so we overheard Dove and Hex talkin' 'bout it with Dove, who also felt some type about her. So once The Dark Cavern opened its doors, me, Larry and Kione snatched her and a friend when they came to Dove's place to check on her. After that, Dove had us snatching bitches left and right." "Did Hex know?" Silence. The two men stared at each other, one wishing he hadn't left his gun in the glove compartment, while the other wished they'd hurry up and let him go already. "Alright, I'm only gonna ask once. Where's this hoe house?" Demanded Mason, hope beating in his chest that he'd soon be reunited with his wife. "The Dark Cavern's in Easton CT."

CHAPTER TWENTY

Omaire hopped in the whip and damn near ran every light getting to Ty's. He yerked up ready to blow the horn, only to see Ty already inside a money green F-150. Nodding, Omaire quickly shot Ty a text askin' if he had everything, meaning weapons. Ty blew the horn in answer, and they were off. Easton was a quaint lil town painted picture perfect with cottage type houses, tree lined streets, and people mowing lawns; while neighbors offered scones and ice tea breaks. Birds sang, children played, it was a far cry from the states capitol city. Nugget sat behind the wheel of a black Ecnoline van, its rear windowless, while the back seats had been yanked out and replaced with two hard benches that held clamps and rings to attach someone to. Hex and Adam were unhappy guests at the moment, sitting with duck tape covering jammed in dirty socks Nugget had used to wipe his Johnson two weeks ago when he'd fucked some broad he'd met at an afterparty. Handcuffs joined the pair whose arms looped thru each other, while ankles were cuffed and run through rings bolted to the vans floor. A huge crate held bags of goodies; grenade launcher, Tek 9's, AK-47's, just to name a few. No music played which scared the unwilling occupants even more as thoughts of what would happen to them once they got to their destination circled like vultures in the sky ready to feast. Adam's thoughts leaned between getting to a hospital and then calling the cops; he was sure he could talk his way out of any situation. Hex's thoughts were geared more towards helping Mason and Nugget, to prove that he'd had no parts of Dove's kidnapping of Taylor. He'd gotten his life right and wanted to live to a ripe old age to enjoy it. Kione shot a quick text to Joe letting him know he didn't feel well and needed him to cover his shift tonight. His plan was to sneak in around midnight and rescue his mother and a few other chicks if they were willing to bounce. If not, oh well. Decision made, Kione felt much better. The past was where it would be left, never to be brought up again while he mended bonds with Taylor; then he'd ask about his father, who he hoped was still alive. Joe responded with an 'okay, no prob' which had a cheese eating grin slid across his face. Midnight. He couldn't wait... "Damn, this one lily white town," bemoaned Ty as he entered Easton's town limits. As they drove past a 'Welcome to Easton, Population 7,490' sign, Ty added, "I wonder how many are of black or other descent." Omaire didn't reply as he was to busy grinding molars everytime Ty spoke in an annoying monotone. After driving around for two hours both were getting pissed at not finding what they sought. "You sure white boy said Easton and not East Haddam or Eastford? Hell, how 'bout Essex and East Hampton?" Ty sarcastically replied. "Kiss m..my ass n..nigga, I..I k..now what I h..heard." Ty laughed, which grated thick chills down Omaire's spine; seemin' to hit every nerve ending along the way. "Fuck h..happened to y..you a..anyway?" Omaire callously asked. "Were y..you b..born that way or s..somethin'?" Ty was used to ignant mofos askin' stupid questions, so he let it roll off his back like duck butter. "Nah, I was shot. Yo ass always stutter?" He volleyed. Of course Omaire immediately felt some type as from the time he started talking he was ridiculed by friends and some family members; so hearing Ty brought back painful images of childhood. Angry, Omaire hissed out a, "F.. fuck you n..nigga." cut across a lane of traffic and pulled into a Shell station. "I..I should've l..left y..yo a..ass wit' yo car w..w.. when it b..broke down. See h..how f..far y..y..yo ass get t..then." Opening car door, Omaire stepped out, slammed the door and marched inside. Ty shook his head at Omaire's bitch move, then lit up a Black & Mild. "So what's the plan?" asked Nugget, turning left on Asmara Way, which was a small street with no sidewalks or light poles, A rabbit shot across the road causing both men to jump in surprise. "Damn, I should've hit that shit and made a stew." Mason chuckled, "Rabbit, I've never had road kill stew before." "Sheeit, when I visited granny every summer down in Alabama, we'd always have possum and whatnot for dinner; and mann let me tell ya, that's some good eating right there." "I'll pass and stick with normal shit like steak, chops n shit." said Mason. Nugget looked back at his guests, "Right or left on Norton Road?" Neither man responded, so Mason pulled Adam's knife, slid between front bucket seats and walked up on Adam and Hex; both's eyes widened in horror. "I only ask once. Since neither answered, hold this, then tell me how you feel." Mason poked both right where thigh and knee met; both howled behind sock taped gags as pain and blood took over. Adam quickly leaned to the right, sat back up, then did it again twice more. "Right Nugget," said Mason. Tears freely ran down Adam's face as he'd now received two injuries, compared to Hex's one. Man he hated Hex's ass right now! "Think I'll just hang out back here til we arrive at our destination." Said Mason before taking a seat on the opposite bench. After what felt like hours Ty and Omaire finally arrived, a long ass winding drive; mostly hidden behind crops of thick trees led them to The Dark Cavern. It hadn't helped that a calf high sign read 'T.D.C.' which they'd driven by twice before noticing it. Now, moments away from rescuing Taylor, both were hype and ready for action. "F..

finally!" Stuttered Omaire. "I h..hate to b..break i..it to you, b..but T..Taylor'll be l..leaving w..wit me." Voicebox at his throat, Ty sucked his teeth. "What eva nigga, just drive. We'll see who she wants soon enough." Five minutes later, Mason, Nugget and company took the turn up the drive; eager to dead whoever stood in their way. Coming round the curve, Nugget stopped a few feet right before coming fully into view. "Fucks that?" Inquired Nugget. Mason stood and grabbed one of the bags, unzipped it and pulled out AK-47, a Glock, and a Beretta then loaded up with extra clips. Nugget jumped out, opened the back door and jingled keys. "Showtime." he sang. Kione raced to The Dark Cavern, he couldn't wait until midnight. Something was telling him to go now to resuce his mother and he wasn't gonna ignore the feeling. Omaire signaled for Ty to wheel his ass round back while he took the front. "See that?" Mason nodded, watching some dude in a wheelchair head around back. "Yep, lets go." A barrel nudge in Hex's back got both who were still handcuffed together moving. Nugget ratcheted rounds, raised a booted foot and kicked in the front door, while simantaneously shooting Omaire three times in neck, chest and torso and down he went, twitching, blood pouring. Nugget quickly looked over his shoulder and advanced inside... So Glenda's ass finally got some courage from tha Wizard and got tha rollin' pin from tha kitchen and snuck it to me. Reba was in tha room chattin' it up wit' Belinda, so I quickly made my way towards tha bathroom to wait on Reba when a loud boom sounded from tha front and back doors. Chile, I thought my heart grew wings and tried to fly right out my breastbone! I hit tha floor, rollin' pin clankin' loudly against tha floor. Joe came runnin', big ass machete in hand, only to hit tha floor inches away when gunfire sang a song against flesh. Screams loudly pierced tha air from tha back; sounded like Reba had met tha same fate as Joe. Fucks goin' on?! Was this a take-over? Had Dove sent them? And where was Glenda? Shit, I'm too young and fly to meet my maker okay. I've still got dicks to suck, balls to gargle n shit, I'm just sayin'. Suddenly all was quiet. Slowly raisin' my head, I winced as gun smoke attacked my nostrils along wit' tha strong scent of blood. A few more shots rang out. Now a bitch ain't gone lie. I've been 'round gunfire my whole life, but tha shit ain't neva been up close and personal where I'm layin' on tha floor; hopin' them shits keep on flyin' right by my black ass. "Taylor!" Time stopped, a'ight. Now I'm hearin' shit, 'cause that sounded like Mason; but it couldn't be. "Taylor, where you at ma!" It was! "Mason! I'm here!" I yelled so loud my vocal cords itched. Best believe a bitch feet grew wings 'cause I was up and racin' down that hall like me and Flo Jo were sisters! And there he was! My boo, tha love of my life! Next thing I know I'm wrapped in strong, muscular arms, I was finally home. Kione pulled up and felt his eyes buck. Naked bitches were running and screaming; one tripped over a prone figure he knew in his gut was dead. Slowly exiting car, Kione strode closer; gazed at the bloody figure and didn't recogonize him, but his face was also covered in blood so it was hard to tell. Heart racing, he started towards the door, ignoring chicks yelling to run the other way. His mother was in there, come hell or high water he wasn't leaving without her when the door opened. Nugget raised his gun ready to lay the little nigga down when Taylor screamed out, "Don't! Wait!" Eyes hard, he glared at dude then walked up and frisked his ass. No weapon, so he relaxed his stance. Mason glared at Kione, then Taylor. Was this little nigglet his wife's side piece? Was that why she'd screamed out don't? "Fuck's going on Taylor, who the fuck is this? And why you don't want his ass down for the count?" Boomed Mason. I don't know what made me yell that shit okay, 'cause here's my chance to get rid of this nigga and my motherly instincts kick in and forbid it. I stared at Kione's ass debating on what to say and how to say it; after all Mason didn't even know I was pregnant when he'd gone away; and now here he stood ready to lay down his flesh and blood to protect me. Ump, I'ma suck tha skin off dat dick later, got my pussy leakin' like a mafucka okay. "No, it's nothin' like that." Sigh. "He's your son, our son Mason." Mason froze except for his eyes that searched from head to toe, he could see the similarities between he, Taylor and himself. They needed to get lost before someone do gooder reported the sounds of gunshots so he refrained from making any comments, at least for now. Mason, Glenda, Kione, and I rode back in Omaire's car, while Nugget loaded up the van with all the hoes before following behind. I was kinda sad to hear Ty and Omaire were no more, but if they're late asses had come sooner, they'd still be alive. Oh well. I'm safe, Glenda's safe, my boo Mason's back, my son's alive; hopefully we can repair our relationship, and after I track down Dove's ass, all will be right in my world.

CHAPTER TWENTY-ONE

'Somethin's wrong.', thought Dove as she stepped on tha elevator in her apartment building. She'd spent four weeks in Polk City Florida, a small ass town scopin' out a building to open up another Dark Cavern since business was so good; but she hadn't heard from Reba or Joe. They knew to call her wit' an update and yet her phone hadn't rung once. Larry had at least done his part and had picked her up from tha airport, dropped her at tha front entrance and went to park. Every night Joe or Larry would stay for a few hours, just to make sure she was straight before callin' it a night. Exitin' on tha eigth floor, Dove walked down carpeted hall to apartment 8G; pulled keys out her purse and unlocked tha door. Tha hairs on her nape rose. She froze in tha doorway, starin' into darkness that was her livin' room, ears tuned for tha slightest sound. Nothin'. Where was her pussycat Taylor? She always came runnin'; and where tha hell was Larry? He should've parked and been upstairs by now.

Five minutes earlier... "You sure?" I blew my boo a kiss. Aww, he's concerned 'bout me; don't be okay. I took months of mind games, starvin' and havin' to let that crazy bitch do things to my body. No way am I sittin' out tha finale to let Mason and Nugget have all tha fun m'kay; 'cause Tay's back and she's got a score to settle. "Positive." Mason smiled all proud n shit, makin' my snacks purr. Ooo, I can't wait to get his ass naked, cause Mason's wieldin' a footlong, wide as a six year old's arm, wit' a fat, juicy, mushroom shaped head dick that he uses oh so well to slay tha pussy, I'm just sayin'. "There they are." Nugget mumbled, eyes glued on a silver Taurus that had pulled up in front of Dove's building. I could see Dove lean from the passenger seat and give Larry a smooch before they pulled into a parking deck that sat to tha buildings left. "Nugget wait for Dove to get inside, then take care of dude. Tay and I are goin' upstairs." "What 'bout me?" asked Kione. Mason glanced at him through rearview mirror. "Sit tight, keep an eye out. If trouble arrives, handle it. Nugget, give him that Glock." Nugget did as told and said, "I'm on it."

Two minutes later.... Damn, my boo ain't lost his touch.

Mason jimmied tha lock and presto! Ump, dis bitch livin' lavish off our backs. Mason used lit phone screen to scan her apartment, when a fuckin' ugly ass tabby cat came outta nowhere, purrin' and rubbin' against my mans legs. Sorry but dis pus' tha only one allowed to touch this okay. Earlier, Mason had given me a foldin' knife; so I nicely flicked it open, bent down and stabbed his ass six quick times; cuffed that neck and walked toward tha kitchen and tossed his ass in a semi full freezer. Dove stepped inside, pulled out her cell and called Larry; makin' sure to leave tha door open for a quick exit. Larry's phone rang until voice mail picked up. "Fuckin' Larry can't do anythin' right," muttered Dove. Downstairs, in a semi lit parkin' deck; Nugget stood beating the hell outta Larry with two pairs of brass knuckles. He'd waited until Larry got out the car, eyes scanning the landscape for any all seeing camera eyes. When Larry strode to the trunk and withdrew a laptop sized bag, he was there to greet him with a punch to upper neck and lower skull. Larry's head wacked the trunks lid with enough force to deeply cut forehead. More blows rained down; solar plexis, kidneys, followed by a silent shot dead center to the back of the head. Gathering some courage, Dove gently moved from in front of her door, then tiptoed into her kitchen wher she kept tha bullets to her gun; which was in the hall closet in her freezer. Using her phone light would alert whoever was in her apartment to her presense, so Dove tried to mentally picture exactly where inside her freezer it was. Only, when she felt inside all she felt was slightly cooling fur. "Aargh!" She screamed, then slapped a hand over her mouth. Heart racing, limbs frozen, Dove felt herself on the brink of hyperventilating as her brain screamed 'Run'! The light flickered on, causing gas to bubble and urine to pool between her legs on the floor. Not wanting to be stabbed in the back, Dove turned eyes widening in surprise, Taylor! Behind her stood a handsome man she'd never seen before. "Surprise!" I taunted, enjoyin' tha fact that just tha sight of me had tha bitch pissin' herself. "T..Taylor! Oh my God, you scared me!" An evil grin slid across my face. "I bet." Mason tossed a stack of papers on the kitchen table. "Have a seat." Dove audibly swallowed, "I..I prefer to stand." "Suit yourself." 'Cause I could care less what tha bitch did, she'd be dead soon. "Sign it; and before you act all clueless, you're turnin' over all assets to moi, includin' bank accounts here and abroad. Hex already did his part, so there's no need to hem and haw on how you can't." Damn it felt good sayin' that okay; and tha look on her face was fuckin' priceless. Too bad I ain't think to snap a quick pic wit' Mason's cell. "And..and if I don't?" Dove spat tryin' to appear hard. Chile please, them days are gone boo okay. Yo best bets to make an introduction wit' tha devil; cause he's stokin' tha fire in yo honor boo, I'm just sayin'. Mason pulled a Glock, flipped off tha safety and used it to point at tha papers. Wobbly legs brought her to tha table; I produced an ink pen, then watched Dove sign her rights away. Checkin' to make sure she'd done as told, I nodded and two shots went off, droppin' her ass like a stone. Unfoldin' knife, which I've grown quite fond of by tha way, I circled tha table and kneeled on tha floor in front of an air gaspin' Dove; shirt hella bloody from shots to stomach and right breast. "Ump, look atchu; assed out and outta breath and time. Rest in hell bitch." I spat, then calmly, slowly, deeply, sliced her fuckin' throat; stood gathered papers, took hubby's hand and walked away without a backward glance. Tha names Taylor James. I'm forty nine and at one time I was called an old freak and I had no problem livin' up to tha name okay. I've fucked, fought and sucked my way through life, stackin' cash, 'cause no one lays wit' greatness fo' free okay. I trusted a bitch I thought had my back and ended up slicin' her fuckin' throat just like I said I would. Yeah, a bitch had enemies but who doesn't, feel me. Its all good though cause my boo, my world, my hubby Mason is back in my arms and trust these streets ain't seen shit yet. Ooow I can't wait to get Cranked Halla.....

THE END

CHAPTER 1

Whoop! Whoop! Police zoom by as I'm exiting Blue's package store. Yeah, there's a package store or two where I stay; but tha actions in Hartford, so that's where I be. It's been awhile since I hung out, so all I'm seein' is new faces out here doin' shit as usual. Hmp, tha faces might change, but bullshit remains the same okay. Bored, I cruise over to China's, y'all remember her, right? My cousin who ain't got tha sense God gave a gnat. Soon as I pull up, all I hear is that mumblin' auto tune mafugga Future. Chile bye, dat boy can't hold a damn tune; but I'd whip dis pussy on him, have him singing crystal clear, holdin' notes and breakin' glass better than Ella herself. Hmp, ask 'bout me boo; a'ite. Shit, I'm just sayin'; cause if ain't nobody gonna tell it like it is, best believe Taylor James will, okay. Anywhoo, dis trick gots a whole cookout, party thang goin' on. Hmp, somebody tell her ass a party ain't a party 'til Taylor strolls thru. Aww sukey, what's this I see; some mafuggin' possibles walkin' round. You know; It's possible I might let you push up, if yo talk game right. It's possible if yo pockets gots more than lint and a few crumbled up bills; and it's possible only if yo tongue games strong and yo dicks long okay. I'm just sayin', don't waste a bitch time, a'ite. I might be older, but I'm like seasoned meat marinating in finger licking juices that'll have you comin' back so much you've gotta unbuckle yo pants. Damn, what was I 'bout to say? Done got all off track picturin' big dicks just a swingin'. Shit, I'm droolin'… A'ite, I'm back. It's been a while and I got a lil excited ya heard; but you tell anybody, and I'll deny that shit. Tha usual "Hey Tay's" and "Sup sexy's" rang out as I make my way in the yard of a yellow, one story home China swears she done bought. Please, unless Section 8 givin' that option now, she need to sit down and shut tha hell up. A look around and I see her at tha grill playin' chef, in apron and all. Makin' note not to touch anythin' her non-cookin' tail made, I walked over. "So, this how you doin' it; havin' cookouts and shit and don't call no damn body?" Flippin' a hamburger patty, she finally glanced up. "Ooh, sorry girl. I'm so busy the shit slipped my mind. Did you bring anything?" 'Wait…what? 'Xplain to me how in the safety pin on a bra strap I'm supposed to bring shit when my black ass ain't know jack 'bout it in tha first place?' "Nah, I didn't."; and with that I got my switch on away from her ass before I went tha hell off. I'm just sayin'. ^

Hmph! Chile, that cookout was a whole mess okay. If the steaks weren't burnt, they were bloody; and last I checked, vampire don't run in my family. Tha potato salad ain't have a lick of potatoes, just mayo, eggs that needed to boil a lil longer, onions and a whole bottle of paprika. Hmph! Don't get me started okay. So, next thing I know, drunk Larry starts arguin' with some dude. Dude smashes his beer bottle upside his head; only Larry didn't fall, them two started scrappin', knockin' shit over and what not. Tha shit was comical. Best believe I grabbed a handful of chips seconds before they toppled to grass, and watched tha show; and hunny they got it crackin'! 'Til Larry tackled his ass atop tha grill. Dude's jheri curl and shirt caught fire. Screamin', he started runnin' round, ignorin' yells to stop, drop and roll. I guess all a dat runnin' ignited it even more, cause there was a loud whoosh and his ass really started cookin'! Best believe it was time to be out, cause I ain't see shit, smell shit, or know shit when the law rolled up. Back home, feet up, a glass of Paulie and Coke in hand; I watched ole cute ass Henry Simmons Jr, better known as detective Baldwin Jones on NYPD Blue, strut all dat sexiness across tha screen. Hmph. I'd sop his ass up like gravy okay; slurp him right on down. Then again, dudes kinda wiry lookin', I might break somethin'. Hell, errbody knows I like meat on my men, a'ite. I ain't tryin' a be poked by a hipbone and shit; I'm just sayin'. Okay 'nough pussy footin' around, let me bring ya nosy asses up to speed on Tay's life, ya heard. My son Kione moved down to Florida with his girl turned wife. I don't really care much for ole Yolanda, aka YoYo; but as long as I don't hear nothin' too crazy on how she treats mines, than we all good. I talk to him at least twice a month, just to check in. Dove also got hitched. Hmph, ain't jack special 'bout tyin' tha knot okay. Trust, when I say never a damn gen, believe it. Shit, it's easy to get into and hard as fuck to get out. I'm still waitin' on shit to be finalized and free any damn day now, unless Mason decides to be difficult. Anywhoo, we parted ways cause he's a lyin', sack of crap; a big ass stankin' bag! That mafugg tried to play me! Me! All along he had a side hoe. Some little skank barely out a trainin' bra he'd met while in prison; and if that wasn't bad enough, lil Ms. Know It All had given him a daughter. Mason ain't know what to say or do. If his hoe had stayed in a chiles place, I would've been none the wiser; but since she made her presence known by tryin' a embarrass greatness, I laid her ass out, called her man and told him where to come collect her. His ass was also back committing robberies. He'd done a few and got caught three months later; why? Cause his toddler ain't know how to keep her trap shut. She bragged, tha haters hated, and bam! There you have it. I heard they threw tha book at Mason. I also heard ole girl been flappin' them lips to any who'll listen that I had Mason's money, and wouldn't turn it over so that she could take care of their child. Bish bye, okay. I must have boo boo tha fool stamped on my forehead to fall for dat hot shit. You wanna know what's crazy, Mason's baby momma's, this chick name Megan, who just so happens to be ole Rosalie's niece. Ain't that some shit?! Rosalie, hmph. Don't even get me started on her, or them two, man sharin' tramps. Rosalie's in the new Nelton Court. Toni and Kelly finally stopped free loadin' and moved out. Who knows, they're probably still sharin' Brick; cause that's what hoes do, okay. I'm just sayin'; cause how many sistas you know out here not only sharin', but scrappin' ova tha dick. I had got a sample to see what tha fuss was all about, and I still don't see it, a'ite. It was a'ite, nothin' to do back flips over; I'm just sayin'; and that's 'bout it. Oh yeah, I've got some new hangin' partnas, Sissy and Royce. Dem my bitches right there, ya heard. I kinda like Royce more, cause she don't give a hoot just like me. I met Sissy at tha Puerto Rican parade. Both her parents speaka the language. She understands it if you speak slow, but speaks not a damn lick. Weird, right? How you know what's bein' said, but can't reply? Shakin' my damn head on that one; and Royce I met at a Big C party. Whoo! Let me say right here and damn now, ain't no party like a Big C party; what what! That big bastard be doin' tha damn thang okay! Anywhoo, Royce was cussin' some chick out cause she bumped her and ain't say xcuse me. Hmph. Dats me all day errday, and twice on

Sunday; thought chu knew! Ask 'bout me bitches, cause I'll still beat a tramp down to tha mafuggin' gristle, I'm just sayin'. And bam, there you have it. Oh snap, I also got tha roster back up and runnin'. Ain't no way I'm a let dese good ole snacks dry up and wither away, a'ite. ^ I hate when a hoe can't read tha damn signs. So what my cars in tha driveway. If I ain't ansa when you rang tha doorbell, or when them dry ass monkey paws raised up and knocked, obviously I ain't wants to be bothered. So, what she do; press her mug against tha glass and start yellin' my govment. Strike two. Dis ain't tha hood, I live in a respectable mafuggin neighborhood. They don't tolerate ghetto shenanigans, and got them boys on speed dial okay. Stompin' to the front door, I yanked it open and snatched China's ass inside by that miniscule ponytail of hers. Shit so short I can see her thoughts, okay. I'm just sayin'. When you know yo shit too short to roll with rice, you don't try and snatch yoself bald tryin' a rock somethin' dat just ain't for you boo, a'ite. Dats like tryin' a suck a four-incher wit' some big ass lips; It ain't gonna happen. "Oww! Girl let my shit go!" She yelped. Hmph, I could barely grip dat shit with my fingernails! "Girl, shut tha hell up. You tha one that came ova here makin' all that damn noise. Now what tha hell you want?" Rubbin' her scalp like I'd snatched her balder than she already was, I watched her have a seat, cross her legs and look round like she's cataloging shit to steal. "Got any Advil, my damn head hurts somethin' awful." Suckin' teeth, I ignored her whinin' ass and glared at her. "Okay, okay. I came to see if I can borrow five hundred. I'll pay you back soon as I get my check." She rushed out. "I look like Webster bank to you?" This fool had tha nerve to nod her melon yes! Grabbin' Newport, I lit up with deep inhale. "And just what do you need it for, pray tell?" Them eyes started bouncin' round like tha furniture had asked tha question and shit. Nervous fingers scratched back of neck, and right then I knew her ass was lying. "Bish bye, I wasn't born last night, or any other night hunnie. You wanna bond yo new boo out for he gets his peanut butter packed." China stiffened, 'damn, Tay's slick ass done peeped game.', judged China. "You got me; but yeah, that's what's up? Can I get that." Lips curled in distaste from how that shit sounded, I stared at her coo coo for Cocoa Puffs tail and laughed so hard I caught a stitch in my damn side. Chile I laughed so hard, not only did tears fall, a stream of pee shot out and dampened my damn drawers; and before y'all get it f'd up, no I don't have bladder problems, and no I don't need to invest in a box, bag, whateva tha hell they come in. Depends. Dats right, I reads minds; and yours 'bout to land yo eye in sleepy town when I shut dat bitch. Ask 'bout me a'ite. Besides, I leave tha wet urine drawers to hoes like Missy; but dats anotha story. "Ahn! Ahn! Wrong! My name ain't Webster boo, or any variation okay; its Taylor. Yeah, we fam, but so tha fuck what dats got to do with tha tea in China? Shit, I ain't fuckin' King's narrow ass. You best hit up tha stroll and do what you do best." Her bottom lip damn near dragged tha ground in response. Shit so long she could take in three dicks, okay. I'm just sayin'. "See, it took a lot for me to come here and ask; and you can't, won't do me a solid. I'd do it for you Tay'." Hmph! Just sad I tell ya; tha hound doggy look, the poked-out lip. Chile, straight pitiful! "Ha! You'd do it for me; that's what you claimed? Hmm, if memory serves, I needed twenty- five measly ass dollars to take tha Greyhound up to Maine when Mason got arrested. You'd just scammed Bonner's for a houseful of furniture, sold it and I couldn't get it. Ooo, and tha time I asked you to go half with me on aunty Barbra's retirement party; member that? You should since dats yo momma." I snapped, cause ole girl's takin' me there a'ite; and once I go there, its ova. See, dis shit right here's why you can't be nice to animals, kids and tha elderly okay; cause all of 'em ain't got tha sense God gave a worm a'ite. With a roll of the eye, China knew better, stood and headed for front door. "That's fucked up. God don't like ugly Taylor; and when your day comes, I'll have a front row seat! Wait one bald ball sac second! I know dis wench ain't just low key threaten my ass cause I won't bond her shiesty, crazy dude out. Before I could stand up, China was out tha door and halfway down tha street. Hmph, I wish I would. King's loony ass got himself in it, let him get himself out, okay!'

Dat nigglets mood shifted like tha wind. One minute he's cool, friendly; tha wind blows and it's all 'stop questionin' him' or he's sittin' on tha curb holdin' a whole conversation with himself loud as hell. Last summer he claimed tha moons glow set his clothes on fire, and set to strippin' in tha middle of a school zone in broad daylight. China sternly told all King wasn't crazy, just mis-understood. Please, dat nigglet needs to just say no to everythin' but water, I'm just sayin'. ^

CHAPTER 2

China I can't stand my cousin. Ole bat always thought she was better at everything, knew everything and that everyone wanted that dried up, gray haired snatch. Sorry about that, the name is China. Remember when Glenda and I got into it on the city bus? Yeah, I knew who the bitch was. I ain't like her ass either. Dove was my bitch. I was rooting for her when she went up against Taylor's ass. Hell, Taylor was damn near tricking until Mason came in the picture and upgraded her broker than broke ass. Mason. Just mentioning that fine man's name gets me horny. That's right, I slobbed all over that big dick he carries around, four days after they tied the knot. Bet her ass ain't know that. And when that Megan chick came out the wood work, my ass did a hand stand! Yes! Yes; and she'd had his daughter to boot! It couldn't get any damn better! Fuck Taylor. I'll come up with the money to bond mines out, cause I know King would do the same for me. ^ -Megan- Incessant crying was giving me the migraine from hell. if I'd known that I'd be stuck broke and alone raising a crying ass kid, I would've been first in line at the abortion clinic. My names Megan. I'm the chick who slid in, got with Mason, saw that green and made sure I'd always be around by giving him a daughter. Sure, I know all about his wife Taylor, but she knew nothing about me; and I liked it that way, at first. I ain't gone lie, I realize now that I messed shit up; out here bragging, showing off the new me. I even made it my business to go to a club where I knew she'd be. I wanted her to know her game ain't as tight as she thought; cause if it was, I wouldn't have stood before her with six- month pregnant belly. Anyway, the shits over now. Mason's locked up, and I'd blew through the money I'd had. Then it came to me, Taylor. She still had plenty of Mason's dough, half of which rightfully belonged to his daughter Masoni. I just wasn't sure how to go about getting my...I mean Masoni's share; but when I did, Taylor James better watch out. ^ The Taste of Hartford is held every year downtown. Restaurants from all over would come and prepare delicious items at expensive ass prices, which were purchasable by ticket only; and that shit right there is why I ain't usually mess with it. The shit was a complete rip off. Two tickets couldn't buy you shit, neither could three; the cheapest item cost six. Them mafuggas knew what they was doin', that's for damn sure. Bastards. Nevertheless, crowds faithfully come. Royce had got on my last nerve, badgerin' a bad bitch like moi to go with her. So to shut her up, I kept it cute in simple capris, off tha shoulder blouse and some Jordans. Tha face as always was beat to tha gawds, okay. Royce of course, was running late, so I hopped on tha city bus cause parkin' downtown is retarded as hell with all them no parkin' from two to five, you will be towed sign bullshit. I ain't got time for tha bullshit; plus, I liked ridin' tha bus. You see some crazy shit, every time, guaranteed. Soon as it pulled up, packed as fuck, I was ready for tha show and I wasn't disappointed. Some dude was being cussed out cause he'd sneakily beat his meat to a teen sittin' in tha seat before him. They was goin' at it; 'til some big ass mofo made his way up front, snatched dick beater by his scrawny neck and commenced to whippin' dat ass! Then these two chicks got into it. Next thing I know, horse hairs flyin' all over tha bus. Tha driver finally had enough, and radioed in for tha police. Chile, damn near tha whole bus turned on her ass when she refused to open bus doors and let tha troublemakers off. They lumped her up real good too, ha! ^ "Damn chick, what took you so long?" Greeted Royce. We shared a laugh after I told her 'bout my bus ride while walkin' down to Constitution Plaza where it was bein' held. "Where's Sissy?" "Girl where else? Home, up under Aiden's ass." "Eww, tmi girl." The Taste was packed! Yess! Momma saw quite a few samples I'd like to taste, and I don't mean food okay. Sheeit, Taylor loves tha buffet a'ite! Why sample one when your choices were roamin' past in sweats, dick just a bouncin'? A few looked like that circumcision went a lil to far up, cause all these twenty twenties saw was balls. Don't get me wrong, cause I'll tea bag them son of bitches. There was a lot of skinny jean wearin' ones too. Brakes! Tha fuck is that shit 'bout? Hmph, balls got to breathe, okay. Got yo shits on a serious lock down, walkin' all stiff legged. I'm just sayin', tha shit ain't cute a'ite. Anywhoo, I tried some bbq from Black Eyed Sally's, and got a slice of cheesecake. A jazz band had set up, while up ahead ice cream was bein' handed out. I definitely would be stoppin', cause errbody knows sweets and dicks are my weakness. Royce tapped my arm. "There goes Country." She wiggled eyebrows. "Sheeit, fuck you tellin' me for? That nigglet still gots Similiac on his breath." Royce burst out laughing. "Hmm, well here he comes. I'll be back, I wanna try a slice of that cake." With a point she took off. Lips curled, I watched Country, real name Damon Hogan, damn near take flight to talk to me. Yes, I like 'em young, but a bitch does have some standards a'ite. So whateva you heard, don't believe it; cause I ain't got no shame in mines, okay. Country's had a crush on me since tha age of fifteen. He was eighteen now and a definite cutie, but it was somethin' tellin' me don't do it. Best believe I learned tha hard way 'bout goin' against that lil voice. "Sup Taylor." A flash of gold grill. Eww nigga, bet yo joints look like popcorn kernels under there. "Hey Country. Who you here with?" Like I gave a flyin' fuck. "Nobody. So whas up; when you gone give yo boy a play? I'm eighteen now." Eager eyes raced up, then down these killa curves (yep, ATL babe!). Hmm, how 'bout neva boo, okay. Shit! No job, no apartment, and from tha look of it, no dingaling all squeezed in them skinny jeans. "Look Country..." "Damn Taylor, you've sunk to a new low since Mason dumped you for me. He's just a kid." Immediately grated on my damn nerves. See, dis tha shit I be talkin' 'bout. It's a good two hundred plus people out here, but she's gotta come for me. Now when I use dat stroller her lil iguana ridin' in and beat tha breaks off a her, I'd be wrong; right? Wrong, cause Megan knows I don't fucks with her. Stay in yo lane boo, okay. Cause you ain't tha first loose pus' to stroll up and try and takes mines; and best believe rat in a stroller or no, if I wanted Mason, I'd have him. Royce walked up, eyed Megan and rolled slanted eyes. "Megan, boo; you lookin' hella broke girl. Strippin' obviously ain't pannin' out for ya."

Her jaw clenched. 'Yess hun, drink all tha fineness that is Taylor Marie James in. You see tha hair, slayed, while you rockin' a tired ass weave that done lifted round tha hairline. Hmp, tha hate is real!' "Fuck you. You only stuntin' cause Mason set yo yam ugly ass up." she snarled, lookin' like an angry ass beaver. 'Ole buck tooth hoe betta recognize for I snap, crackle and knock her ass out, okay. Ask 'bout me, cause I luv beatin' ass; and just cause you've got yo baby vulture with you means jack. I don't do kids boo, and will happily kick that shit right in traffic.' "Tay', who the hell is this? You got beef?" Country's weak ass had disappeared, which I was grateful for. Smilin', I answered with a, "Nah. Megan here is just one of my hatin' ass fans." Royce burst out laughing; only to wince when her eyes landed on tha creature inside stroller. I could tell she was dyin' to say somethin'. "Fuck all this back and forth bullshit. Masoni needs things, things I feel you should handle, since your living type lovely on my man's dough." She spat. Eyes wide, Royce snarled, "Aw hell naw! Chop this tramp in the throat; fuck she think this is!" 'See, that's why Royce my bitch! Maybe I was in a givin' mood, but I gave her ass a pass; her second. There won't be a third. "Let's go Royce. I'm sure I'll see Megan's ass again." And with that we walked off. ^ -Megan- Fuck! Fuck! Fuck! I can't stand Taylor! I screamed so damn loud my throat itched, while Masoni chewed on her index finger. I've tried breaking her out of that nasty shit. I used hot and tobacco sauce, which ain't stop shit. I saw all over her wrinkly face that she had some crazy crap she wanted to let fly 'bout my seed with her husband, well ex. Then, her friend gone stroll up like she's all big and bad; like I'm 'posed to be scared with her, "You got beef?" Ooo, I'm scared; not! Fucking with me she'll get her skull cracked. I think it's time me and Masoni go pay her daddy a damn visit. ^

CHAPTER 3

"C'mon y'all, let's do this before the tickets are all sold out." Whined Sissy. Lord knows I hate whinin'; but from a grown ass woman, tha shits annoyin' with all capital damn letters. She wanted me and Royce to accompany her to some reggae fest out in Danbury. Now errbody knows I love me some reggae music, but them white folks out there as bad as bein' in Wallingford, and I ain't tryin' a go to jail; cause somebody got it f'd up, my ass whoopin's don't discriminate, I'm just sayin' "Whose performing?" Asked Royce as she chomped on grapes. "Hella peeps. C'mon y'all, let's get out of Hartford, ain't shit to do here." Anotha whine. 'Hmph, she just don't know, her ass is pushin' it. Shit, she only wanna hang out cause her she-male mad at her.' "Fuck it. Let's go Tay', we ain't doing nothing." True. Standin', we headed out and made Sissy, who hated driving on the highway, get behind tha wheel. First stop, tha package store. ^ -Megan- An art deco style front, and three hundred and forty-eight acres of lush hills gave Club Fed aka FCI Danbury (Federal Correctional Institute), a country club look. Handball, tennis courts, soccer field, baseball diamond, and a running track took up space at the medium security prison. Parking, eyes wide in awe at picturesque view, quickly narrowed in irritation when her Camry not only backfired, but tried to restart after being turned off. A few heads turned in my direction, angering me even more. Lugging Masoni on hip, I made my way inside, amazed at what I saw. My ex Donald had been locked, and when I went to see him up in Somers, a huge damn rat ran across the visiting room floor. Visits were behind plexiglass, which was dirty and scratched, and half the phones didn't work; but here, the floors were so clean I could eat off them. Even the guards were pleasant! The shit was mind boggling! After being approved for the visit, I took Masoni to the bathroom, then pulled two balloons from my pussy and placed them inside my mouth; one on each side of jaw. Washed my hands, and exited just as they called Mason's name. Damn, they weren't slow either. I can get used to this! Not even two minutes later, here came my man. My heart picked up speed, nipples peeked, and my clit thumped. That's how I knew it was love, cause no man had ever done that to me before. Yeah, Mason's a walking dreamboat. Tall, handsome, rich, horse dick, and built like a solid oak tree. Mason's arms wrapped round, gave a squeeze and I swear I came right there. After, he scooped up Masoni and peppered her cute lil face with kisses, causing her giggles to ring out. As soon as ass met seat, I went in. Fuck pleasantries for real! "I need money." I swear I heard crickets as I waited for him to tell me where he'd stashed a 'just in case' fund. Instead, what I got was, "Where's the money I left at the house?" Shit. What do I say? Am I gonna be honest and admit I blew it on a bunch of trivial bullshit? Or, do I lie and play the sympathy card? "We do have a child Mason, a growing one. Masoni's growing like a weed, plus she's in daycare, which isn't free by a long shot." Can you believe his ass had the gall to roll his damn eyes; like me asking for money to take care of his child was a problem. "Gone." "Gone. I left you enough cash to leave you straight until I discharged. How the hell you spend $300,000?" I fucked around and swallowed the damn balloons from the evil look he threw my way. Nervous, I gazed around, sighed and said, "Arguing won't bring it back Mason. The money's gone. I need money to take care of Masoni. Do you have it or not Mason?" He hesitated, then, "Not." I knew his ass was lying. "Cool. What about Taylor, can you call her?" He mirthlessly laughed. "You're joking, right? You really think my wife will give you money if I call her and ask her to give it to you?" The way he put it did sound pretty stupid. "For the record, she's your ex; and yes, I'm serious. I know you Mason, and I'm sure you left the wicked bitch a nicely cushioned nest egg." "Five minutes remaining!" Yelled a c/o, pissing me off because things weren't going my way. "Listen Megan, you need to get a j-o-b. Taylor's money belongs to Taylor. She sold some properties, invested and is set. You need to let that shit go and do what needs to be done to make ends meet." I wanted to shout, 'that's what I'm trying to do!' The visit ended before I could say anything. I know one thing, I don't give a damn what Mason said. Taylor's the answer, and in time I'd figure it out. In the mean time I needed my old stripper job back. ^

BE ON THE LOOKOUT FOR

COUGER IIII

The Final Book of the Couger Series

ABOUT
THE AUTHOR

New York Times & International Best Selling Author Billie Dureyea Shell was born in Compton California and now lives in Ladera Heights with his wife and kids who he loves to spend time with.

He is the Owner of several properties in the Los Angeles area and gives back to his community by providing low income housing to those who need it.

He stated "It doesn't matter where you at or where you from it's what you do with your time. There's nothing you can't do if you put your mind to it".